Heather Freeman &
Edward D. Andrews

THIRTEEN REASONS WHY YOU SHOULD KEEP LIVING

When Hope and Love Vanish?

THIRTEEN REASONS WHY YOU SHOULD KEEP LIVING

When Hope and Love Vanish

Edward D. Andrews &
Heather Freeman

Christian Publishing House
Cambridge, Ohio

Copyright © 2017 Edward D. Andrews & Heather Freeman

All rights reserved. Except for brief quotations in articles, other publications, book reviews, and blogs, no part of this book may be reproduced in any manner without prior written permission from the publishers. For information, write,

support@christianpublishers.org

Unless otherwise stated, Scripture quotations are from Updated American Standard Version (UASV) Copyright © 2022 by Christian Publishing House

THIRTEEN REASONS WHY YOU SHOULD KEEP LIVING: When Hope and Love Vanish by Edward D. Andrews

ISBN-10: 1945757477

ISBN-13: 978-1945757471

Table of Contents

Book Description 7

Preface 8

INTRODUCTION Four Personal Accounts: The Stories of Hope...10

THIRTEEN REASONS TO KEE LIVING: Navigating Hope in Times of Despair 14

REASON 1 Because Things Will Change Soon 17

REASON 2 Because There Is Help 20

REASON 3 Because There Is Hope 24

REASON 4 Because Your Feelings Do Not Have to Control You 30

REASON 5 Because Others Do Not Define Who You Are or Who You Will Be 34

REASON 6 Because Death Does Not Get Revenge on Those Who Hurt You 38

REASON 7 Because Your Pain Is Not Permanent 42

REASON 8 Because you Can Control Your Life 46

REASON 9 Because Mental Difficulties Can Be Controlled and Overcome..50

REASON 10 Because Loneliness is But Momentary 54

REASON 11 Because Substance Abuse Can Be Overcome 58

REASON 12 Because Bullying and Cyberbullying Can Be Prevented...62

REASON 13 Because Sexual Abuse Need Not Be a Lifetime of Pain 68

CHALLENGED SOULS 1 How Can I Overcome My Depression? 72

CHALLENGED SOULS 2 How Can I Overcome My Anxiety? 76

CHALLENGED SOULS 3 How Can I Cope with This Constant Sadness? 80

CHALLENGED SOULS 4 Protecting Children from Woke Ideological Education: A Biblical Perspective 84

CHALLENGED SOULS 5 Help for Those Who Are Struggling with Transgender Ideology? 97

CHALLENGED SOULS 6 What Does the Bible Say About Transgenderism and Cross-Dressing? 105

CHALLENGED SOULS 7 GENDER IDENTITY: Alternative Lifestyles—Does God Approve? 112

CHALLENGED SOULS 8 Finding Peace Amidst Chaos: A Guide for Today's Youth 123

Bibliography 127

Book Description

In an age rife with challenges, from internal emotional struggles to external pressures, teens and young adults are often caught in the crossfire, grappling with despair, loneliness, and confusion. "THIRTEEN REASONS WHY YOU SHOULD KEEP LIVING: When Hope and Love Vanish" serves as a beacon of hope, shining light amidst the shadows of life's most daunting trials.

Drawing from the wellspring of faith, Biblical truths, and the wisdom of seasoned counseling, this transformative book offers thirteen compelling reasons for choosing life, even when the horizon seems endlessly dark. From the promise of change, the availability of help, to the powerful assertion that personal pain is not permanent, each reason is a testament to God's unwavering love and the intrinsic value of every individual.

Additionally, the "CHALLENGED SOULS" section delves deep into specific challenges that today's youth face, including depression, anxiety, and the complexities of gender identity. This segment provides Biblically grounded guidance, offering clarity and support amidst societal confusion.

"THIRTEEN REASONS WHY YOU SHOULD KEEP LIVING" isn't merely a book—it's a lifeline, an anchor for those adrift in the tumultuous seas of modern life. For anyone on the verge of surrendering to despair, this tome serves as a heartfelt reminder that, with faith and perseverance, there is always a reason to keep living.

Preface

As we sat down to pen this book, the weight of the task ahead weighed heavily on our shoulders. The world has changed at an unprecedented pace, bringing with it challenges and trials that many of our young people grapple with daily. The issues facing today's youth are vast and varied, often leading to feelings of despair and hopelessness. It is with this backdrop that "THIRTEEN REASONS WHY YOU SHOULD KEEP LIVING" was born.

This isn't just another self-help book or a guidebook filled with platitudes. Instead, it's an earnest attempt to reach out to those standing at life's crossroads, searching for answers and hope. Drawing from the unchanging truths of the Bible, real-life experiences, and the insights gained from years of counseling, the ensuing pages are a testament to the resilience of the human spirit and God's unwavering love.

The thirteen reasons highlighted in this book are more than mere words; they're lifelines. They are reminders that even in our darkest moments, light can break through. While the challenges and issues explored in the "CHALLENGED SOULS" section may be specific and contemporary, the principles and guidance are timeless, rooted in age-old wisdom.

We've had the privilege of listening to countless stories—stories of heartbreak, stories of redemption, stories of faith rediscovered and hope reclaimed. It's my sincere hope that as you journey through these pages, you'll find a piece of your own story and recognize that there's always a reason to persevere.

Thank you for letting us be a part of your journey. Our prayer is that you'll close this book with a renewed sense of purpose, a strengthened faith, and the realization that your life, with all its ups and downs, is worth living.

Edward D. Andrews

(AS in Criminal Justice, BS in Religion, MA in Biblical Studies, and MDiv in Theology) is CEO and President of Christian Publishing House. He has authored over 220+ books. In addition, Andrews is the Chief Translator of the Updated American Standard Version (UASV).

Heather Freeman

Graduated Missouri State University with a Bachelor of Science degree in Clinical Psychology in 2011 and went on to complete her Masters of Arts degree at Forest Institute of Professional Psychology in 2013. She currently works as a therapist at Lakeland Behavioral Health Systems, where she has been employed since 2009, using Cognitive Behavioral Therapy to treat children and adolescents suffering from various mood, conduct, trauma, and attachment disorders.

Edward D. Andrews

INTRODUCTION Four Personal Accounts: The Stories of Hope

At the heart of humanity lies an intrinsic desire for connection, understanding, and solace. When faced with adversity, we naturally seek out stories that resonate with our experiences, hoping to find glimmers of hope amidst the storms we face. This book is a testament to that very human longing—a bridge between shared trials and collective triumphs.

To truly understand the significance of the thirteen reasons why one should keep living, we must first delve into the lived experiences of those who have grappled with the tempests of despair, only to emerge stronger, wiser, and more resolute. Here, in this introduction, we will journey through four personal accounts—stories that echo the complexities of modern challenges but also illuminate the path to hope.

From Anna, a teen battling the claws of depression; to Michael, who faced intense bullying both offline and online; to Clara, grappling with gender identity in a world that often misunderstands; and finally to Samuel, who sought refuge in substances to numb his pain, we will uncover the profound depths of their struggles and the soaring heights of their victories.

These stories aren't mere anecdotes; they are powerful testimonies. They remind us that even when faced with overwhelming odds, with faith as our anchor, and with a community of support, we can navigate the turbulent waters of life. These accounts serve as a foundation for the ensuing chapters, setting the stage for the in-depth exploration of each reason to keep living.

As you engage with these narratives, let them be a mirror, reflecting both the vulnerabilities and the indomitable strength that exists within each of us. Let them serve as a reminder that, no matter the magnitude of our battles, hope is never out of reach.

Four Personal Accounts: The Stories of Hope

The following are the raw, unfiltered accounts of four teenagers who have faced immense challenges in their lives. These are their words, punctuated by the authenticity of their experiences. These young individuals have walked paths similar to yours, and through sharing, they hope to shed light on the dark tunnels you might be navigating.

Troubled Teen One

Growing up, I lived under the illusion that my aunt was my mother. I had no inkling of the existence of my biological parents until the age of ten, and the circumstances under which I finally met them were far from ideal. However, the true silver lining in my tumultuous story is the unexpected love and care I received from my grandparents. They became the pillars of strength I so desperately needed. Through every setback, they stood by me, reminding me of my worth and encouraging me to rise above my past. I've learned to be patient and resilient, trusting that brighter days await even after the stormiest nights.

Troubled Teen Two

I'm writing this not as a mere observer, but as someone who has felt the crushing weight of abuse and the deceptive allure of ending it all. Believe me when I say, I understand. The pain, the isolation, the feeling of utter hopelessness—I've been there. However, taking that irreversible step isn't the solution. There are people who care about you deeply, even if it doesn't seem so now. Your life has immense value, and your story, though filled with chapters of pain, can turn into a testament of resilience and hope. Please, stay with us, and let us journey towards healing together.

Troubled Teen Three

Life for me was a tumultuous roller-coaster ride, marked by feelings of extreme isolation despite being surrounded by peers. Falling prey to the treacherous grasp of peer pressure, I donned various masks, hoping to fit in. Yet, the authentic 'me' felt increasingly lost. However, a turning point came in my life when I realized the value of genuine connections over mere popularity. True friends, though few, proved more valuable than a fleeting crowd. Embrace your uniqueness, and remember, your individuality is your superpower.

Troubled Teen Four

My early years were marked by a lack of social skills, making every interaction a challenge. Though I later gained friends and even a romantic relationship, the void within remained. I felt as if I was on a constant quest for identity, trying to mold myself to fit into the expectations of others. However, a revelation dawned upon me: my worth wasn't dependent on the number of people I surrounded myself with, but the quality of those relationships. Today, I'm surrounded by a few, yet genuine friends, and that's what truly matters. Remember, the journey to self-discovery might be long and filled with hurdles, but the destination is worth every struggle.

Edward D. Andrews

THIRTEEN REASONS TO KEE LIVING: Navigating Hope in Times of Despair

Amidst the tumultuous waves of adolescent challenges, it's no surprise that many young souls grapple with thoughts of ending their precious lives. Their reasons resonate with pain, confusion, and an overwhelming sense of loneliness. Presented here are true accounts of such struggles and an urging to see life through a renewed lens of hope and perseverance.

Real Stories, Genuine Struggles

Emily, 16: Overwhelmed with feelings of hopelessness, incessant bullying, and a daunting loneliness.

James, 17: Confronting his same-sex attraction in solitude, grappling with isolation and self-identity.

Ethan, 14: Watching helplessly as domestic violence shatters the peace of his household.

Abigail, 13: Perpetually striving for parental approval, perpetually feeling like she's falling short.

Today's grim statistic reveals a chilling truth: suicide stands as the *second leading cause of death* for those between the ages of 10-24. Alarmingly, this surpasses deaths from ailments like cancer, heart disease, and AIDS combined. While society in the 1980s and 1990s witnessed a declining trend in suicides, today's world presents a stark contrast. Why?

THIRTEEN REASONS WHY YOU SHOULD KEEP LIVING

We can attribute some of the blame to the profound influences today's youth are exposed to. The fast-paced world of internet, relentless social media tools, and an array of entertainment choices ranging from music to reality TV can distort perceptions, diluting core values. Celebrities like the Kardashians command attention, inadvertently defining young individuals' self-worth. Moreover, terms like "sexting" and shows that portray dysfunctional families and alternative lifestyles as the norm further muddle the moral compass. This modern world, while technologically advanced, often leaves its young denizens feeling more isolated and pressured than ever.

Shaping Perception: The Core Challenge

Amid these challenges lies a fundamental truth: it isn't the problems, pressures, and pains that push one to the brink, but rather, *how one perceives them*. Thus, reshaping this perception can significantly alter one's response to life's challenges. Every youth needs to realize that their present adversity is temporary, and with the right support, understanding, and resilience, a brighter future awaits.

Why Continue?

Madison may appear as the epitome of youthful happiness to many, but beneath her cheerful exterior lies a deep abyss of despair. Such stories are far too common. Many young individuals cannot fathom ending their lives but feel trapped in their existent reality, yearning for an accidental escape. They view death as a reprieve, not the enemy.

This book aims to shift this perception, emphasizing not just one, but *thirteen compelling reasons to embrace life*. Just as the series "Thirteen Reasons Why" outlined reasons for its protagonist's tragic end, "Thirteen Reasons to Keep Living" aspires to offer hope, strength, and a renewed zest for life.

Edward D. Andrews

Embark on this journey. Discover not just one, but many reasons to keep living. Embrace hope. Embrace life.

REASON 1 Because Things Will Change Soon

Life is a remarkable journey, filled with highs and lows, joys and sorrows. There's an ancient saying, "This too shall pass," and it holds a profound truth that speaks to the core of human experience. When we find ourselves in moments of despair, the overwhelming emotions can blind us from seeing the bigger picture. It's easy to feel that the pain is permanent, the darkness unending. However, one of the most profound truths of human existence is that change is the only constant. Therefore, when you find yourself thinking there's no way out, always remember: things will change soon.

The Nature of Time and Change

Change is embedded in the fabric of time. Each moment moves forward, bringing new experiences, challenges, and opportunities. No matter how dark the night, the dawn will break. And with that dawn, there is a promise of a new day, a fresh start, and a chance for things to be different.

Scripture reminds us of the transient nature of our troubles. In 2 Corinthians 4:17, Paul writes, "*For our light affliction, which is for the moment, works for us more and more exceedingly an eternal weight of glory.*" This passage doesn't minimize the pain of the present but instead offers perspective. Our current struggles are temporary compared to the eternal glory that awaits us.

Life's Seasons

Just as nature has its seasons, so do our lives. There are times of growth (spring), times of joy and abundance (summer), times of reflection and letting go (autumn), and times of rest and seeming barrenness (winter). Each season holds its own value, and each is necessary for the fullness of life.

Ecclesiastes 3:1 reminds us, "*For everything there is a season, and a time for every purpose under heaven.*" If you find yourself in winter, remember that spring, with its promise of new life and growth, is just around the corner.

The Power of Hope

Hope is the anchor of the soul. Even in the most trying times, hope can shine a light, illuminating a path forward. Hope is not wishful thinking but a confident expectation of good things to come. As Christians, our hope is anchored in the promises of God. Romans 15:13 says, "*Now may the God of hope fill you with all joy and peace in believing, that you may abound in hope, through the power of the Holy Spirit.*"

God's promises are sure and steadfast. Even when circumstances seem bleak, we can trust in His Word. He has promised never to leave or forsake us (Hebrews 13:5) and to be close to the brokenhearted (Psalm 34:18).

Facing Challenges with Faith

Faith is a potent tool in the face of adversity. It's not about denying the reality of your feelings or your situation, but rather trusting that God has a plan and that good can come out of even the most challenging situations. James

1:2-4 encourages us, "*Consider it all joy, my brothers, when you encounter various trials, knowing that the testing of your faith produces endurance. And let endurance have its perfect result, so that you may be perfect and complete, lacking in nothing.*"

Your trials are shaping you, refining you, and preparing you for the plans God has for your life. By facing your challenges with faith, you allow God to work in and through you, bringing about change and growth.

Your Story Matters

Every individual has a unique story, and every chapter of that story holds significance. If you are going through a difficult chapter now, it's crucial to remember that this is not the end of your story. By choosing to keep living, you give yourself the chance to experience new chapters filled with love, healing, growth, and purpose.

Your story has the power to inspire, uplift, and offer hope to others. By overcoming today's challenges, you can be a beacon of hope for others going through similar situations in the future.

In Conclusion

Life, with all its unpredictability, guarantees one thing: change. No situation, no matter how dire, is permanent. With faith, hope, and time, circumstances shift, pain fades, and new opportunities arise.

When despair clouds your vision, cling to the promise of a new day and the unwavering truths of Scripture. Embrace the hope that God offers, and trust that things will change soon. Your life has immense value, and the world needs the unique gifts and perspective you bring. Choose to keep living, for your story is still unfolding, and the best chapters may yet be ahead.

REASON 2 Because There Is Help

In the midst of despair and isolation, it might seem like you are entirely alone. Yet, one of the most comforting truths, both in the natural and spiritual realms, is that help is available. You are not alone. You do not need to navigate the complexities of your emotions and circumstances by yourself. *There is help, and it comes in various forms,* ready to provide the support, understanding, and guidance you may need.

God's Ever-Present Help

First and foremost, as Christians, we believe in an all-knowing, all-loving God who is always available for us. The Psalmist writes in Psalm 46:1, "*God is our refuge and strength, a very present help in trouble.*" This isn't a distant, detached deity but a personal, loving Creator who knows every hair on our heads and every pain in our hearts.

When we cry out to Him in our distress, He listens. Even if you feel like your prayers are just bouncing off the ceiling, they are reaching the ears of a compassionate God. The beauty of this relationship is that, no matter the hour or the depth of despair, *God is an ever-present help.*

The Church and Community

The Christian community, the body of Christ, exists not only for worship and teaching but also for fellowship and support. Galatians 6:2 urges us to, "*Bear one another's burdens, and so fulfill the law of Christ."* The church, when functioning in love and unity, can be a sanctuary for the hurting.

If you're struggling, reach cut to a trusted individual in your church community – be it a pastor, elder, youth leader, or a mature believer. The beauty of the church is that it's filled with people who have faced various challenges and have testimonies of God's grace and deliverance. By sharing your struggles, you allow others the privilege to walk alongside you, pray with you, and support you.

Professional Counseling

While the spiritual dimension is crucial, there are times when professional help is necessary. Christian counselors and therapists are trained to address the emotional, psychological, and spiritual aspects of our being. They can offer coping strategies, provide insights into underlying issues, and give a safe space to express your feelings.

It's important to remember that seeking professional help isn't a sign of weak faith or lack of trust in God. Instead, it's a proactive step towards healing and wholeness. God has equipped counselors and therapists with the skills and knowledge to assist those in distress. Proverbs 11:14 says, "*Where there is no guidance, a people falls, but in an abundance of counselors there is safety.*"

Support Groups

There are numerous support groups, both within and outside the church community, that cater to specific needs and challenges. These groups provide a communal setting where individuals can share their experiences, offer advice, and provide comfort to one another. In such environments, it's often comforting to realize that you're not alone in your struggles. Others have been where you are and have found ways to cope and thrive.

Family and Friends

Often, the immediate circle of family and friends can offer invaluable support. They know you, care for you, and are invested in your well-being. Even if they may not understand everything you're going through, their presence and willingness to listen can be a significant source of comfort.

While it might be challenging to open up, especially if you fear judgment or misunderstandings, expressing your feelings to someone you trust can alleviate the weight of your burdens.

Online Resources and Helplines

In our digital age, numerous resources are available online, from articles to forums to helplines. Christian organizations and ministries often provide resources tailored to believers facing various challenges. If you're not ready to speak to someone face-to-face, starting with an anonymous helpline or an online forum can be a beneficial first step.

In Conclusion

Life's challenges, especially during the turbulent teen years, can be overwhelming. But it's crucial to remember that you don't have to face them alone. There is a vast network of help, both spiritual and practical, waiting to assist you.

THIRTEEN REASONS WHY YOU SHOULD KEEP LIVING

Reaching out might seem daunting, but taking that step can lead to healing, restoration, and renewed hope. Whether it's turning to God in prayer, confiding in a trusted friend, joining a support group, or seeking professional counseling, numerous avenues of help are available.

Your life, with its potential, dreams, and purpose, is invaluable. When you're in the depths of despair, remember: *Because there is help, there is hope.* Choose to reach out, to seek that help, and to continue your journey with the support and love that is available to you.

REASON 3 Because There Is Hope

In the darkest hours, when life feels overwhelming and burdens seem insurmountable, the flame of hope can pierce through the shadows, providing a beacon of light. Hope is not mere optimism or wishful thinking; it is a profound assurance and expectation that things can and will get better. For every individual, especially teens navigating the challenges of growth, relationships, identity, and purpose, understanding and holding onto hope is paramount.

Hope: A Biblical Perspective

The Christian faith is intrinsically tied to hope. From the Old Testament prophecies pointing to a coming Messiah to the New Testament's fulfillment in Jesus Christ, hope has always been a cornerstone.

Romans 15:4 tells us, "*For whatever was written in former days was written for our instruction, that through endurance and through the encouragement of the Scriptures we might have hope.*" The Scripture is a testament to God's faithfulness throughout generations, a testament that serves to fortify our hope.

God's Promises: The Anchor of Our Hope

One of the most profound sources of hope for a believer is the promises of God. These are not mere words but covenants from an unchanging and faithful God. In Hebrews 6:19, we read, "*We have this as a sure and steadfast anchor of the soul, a hope that enters into the inner place behind the curtain.*" This anchor is based on God's promises and the finished work of Jesus Christ.

When you face challenges, doubts, or despair, reflecting on these promises can rekindle hope. God's promise to never leave nor forsake us (Hebrews 13:5), to work all things together for good (Romans 8:28), and to give us a future and a hope (Jeremiah 29:11) are just a few of the assurances that can rejuvenate our spirit.

Hope in Jesus: Our Living Hope

Our Savior, Jesus Christ, is often described as our "living hope." 1 Peter 1:3 says, "*Blessed be the God and Father of our Lord Jesus Christ! According to his great mercy, he has caused us to be born again to a living hope through the resurrection of Jesus Christ from the dead.*"

This "living hope" signifies that our hope is not based on circumstances, feelings, or human effort, but on the person and work of Jesus Christ. His resurrection assures us of victory over death, sin, and every challenge we might face.

Hope and Resilience

Hope breeds resilience. The belief that there's a brighter tomorrow, that our current trials are temporary, can empower individuals to endure and overcome. Resilience doesn't mean the absence of pain but the ability to persevere through it.

Paul, who faced numerous hardships, found hope in the midst of his trials. He wrote in 2 Corinthians 4:16-17, "*So we do not lose heart. Though our outer self is wasting away, our inner self is being renewed day by day. For this light momentary affliction is preparing for us an eternal weight of glory beyond all comparison."*

Hope Inspires Action

Hope is not passive. It's a powerful motivator that can inspire action. If you believe things can improve, you're more likely to take steps towards positive change. This might mean seeking help, connecting with loved ones, engaging in activities you love, or diving deeper into your faith.

The Role of Community in Nurturing Hope

We were never meant to walk through life alone. The Christian community plays a crucial role in nurturing and reaffirming hope. Through fellowship, prayer, worship, and the sharing of testimonies, believers can uplift and encourage one another.

Hearing stories of how others overcame similar challenges, how they witnessed God's intervention in dire situations, can ignite hope in our hearts. And, in times when our hope wavers, the community can hold onto hope for us, interceding and supporting until we find our footing again.

Cultivating a Hopeful Perspective

Cultivating a hopeful perspective requires intentionality. Surrounding yourself with positive influences, immersing in the Word of God, maintaining a prayerful life, and practicing gratitude can all foster a hopeful mindset.

Also, remember that it's okay to seek professional help or counseling to address feelings of hopelessness. Sometimes, external perspectives, especially from trained professionals, can provide tools and strategies to rebuild hope.

The Unseen Potential of Tomorrow

Every challenge faced, every tear shed, and every prayer whispered shapes the individual you are becoming. The trials of today are refining you, preparing you for the blessings and responsibilities of tomorrow. While it might be difficult to envision now, tomorrow holds potential experiences, relationships, joys, and successes that can transform your life in ways you've never imagined.

Scripture reminds us in 1 Corinthians 2:9, "*But, as it is written, 'What no eye has seen, nor ear heard, nor the heart of man imagined, what God has prepared for those who love him.'*" This verse underscores the wondrous plans God has for His children, many of which remain unseen until their appointed time.

Embracing the Journey

Life is not just about destinations but also the journey. Each phase, even the painful ones, contributes to the tapestry of your life. By embracing hope, you are choosing to trust that the journey has value and that every step, even the uncertain ones, leads you closer to your God-given destiny.

Passing the Torch of Hope

Your personal journey of hope doesn't only benefit you. As you navigate life's challenges with a hopeful spirit, you become a beacon for others. Your testimony, your story of perseverance and faith, can ignite hope in someone else's heart. In this way, hope is not just personal; it's communal. By choosing hope, you're not only impacting your life but potentially the lives of countless others who witness your journey.

The Timeless Assurance

In the midst of changing seasons, evolving circumstances, and shifting emotions, there's a timeless assurance that believers can cling to: God's love and faithfulness. Lamentations 3:22-23 proclaims, "*The steadfast love of the Lord never ceases; his mercies never come to an end; they are new every morning; great is your faithfulness.*" This unwavering love is the foundation of our hope.

In Conclusion

Hope is not a fleeting emotion; it's a steadfast anchor. It's the assurance that, no matter the trials, God is in control and has a purposeful plan for each of us. For every teen facing despair, the message is clear: *Because there is hope, there is a future worth living for.*

Life, in all its unpredictability, holds promise, potential, and purpose. Every sunrise heralds a new day, filled with opportunities and experiences yet to be discovered. Even when storm clouds gather, and nights seem endless, the dawn inevitably breaks, illuminating a world rife with possibilities.

THIRTEEN REASONS WHY YOU SHOULD KEEP LIVING

For every teen feeling trapped in the darkness of despair, it's crucial to remember this: darkness is not the end; it's merely a tunnel, and there's light on the other side. Because there is hope, every challenge can be surmounted, every wound can be healed, and every dream can be realized.

Hope is more than just a concept; it's a lifeline. It's the gentle whisper in the night saying, "Hold on, for brighter days are ahead." Embrace this hope, let it anchor your soul, and watch as it transforms not just your present, but your future as well. Remember, *Because there is hope, there is a future worth living for.*

REASON 4 Because Your Feelings Do Not Have to Control You

Feelings are a powerful aspect of our human experience. They can be beautiful and uplifting, filling us with joy, love, and excitement. But they can also be overwhelming, confusing, and distressing, especially when they seem to pull us into depths of despair. As teens navigate the complexities of growth, self-discovery, relationships, and societal pressures, emotional turbulence can be intense. Yet, an essential truth to grasp is this: while feelings are real and valid, *they do not have to dictate our actions or define our identity.*

Understanding the Nature of Feelings

Feelings are natural responses to stimuli, situations, thoughts, or interactions. They can be fleeting or persistent, intense or mild. But importantly, feelings are not always indicators of objective truth. Just because we *feel* something doesn't necessarily make it an accurate reflection of reality.

Jeremiah 17:9 reminds us, "*The heart is deceitful above all things, and desperately sick; who can understand it?*" This verse highlights the idea that our feelings, emerging from our hearts, can sometimes mislead us.

Feelings vs. Facts

One of the foundational steps in preventing feelings from overwhelming control is differentiating between feelings and facts. While your feelings are genuine experiences, they aren't always grounded in reality.

For example, feeling unloved or unwanted in a moment of distress doesn't negate the truth that you are cherished by God and valued by many in your life. Romans 8:38-39 assures us, "*For I am sure that neither death nor life, nor angels nor rulers, nor things present nor things to come, nor powers, nor height nor depth, nor anything else in all creation, will be able to separate us from the love of God in Christ Jesus our Lord.*" This passage underscores a fact that remains constant, regardless of fluctuating feelings.

Taking Control: Capturing Every Thought

The Bible provides guidance on managing our thoughts and feelings. 2 Corinthians 10:5 states, "*We destroy arguments and every lofty opinion raised against the knowledge of God, and take every thought captive to obey Christ.*" By intentionally capturing and assessing our thoughts, we can determine if they align with truth or if they are based on fleeting feelings.

For instance, if a thought arises like "Nobody cares about me," before accepting it as truth, challenge it. Reflect on times when you felt cared for or loved, or consider the consistent love God offers. Reframing thoughts can significantly impact the resulting feelings.

Feelings Are Not Final

It's crucial to remember that feelings change. Today's despair can give way to tomorrow's joy. The anxiety of a moment can transform into the peace of another. Psalm 30:5b states, "*Weeping may tarry for the night, but joy comes with the morning.*" This Psalmist's reflection offers solace in the knowledge that emotional states are temporary.

The Role of Prayer and Meditation

In the midst of emotional turmoil, prayer and meditation on Scripture can be grounding. Philippians 4:6-7 advises, "*Do not be anxious about anything, but in everything by prayer and supplication with thanksgiving let your requests be made known to God. And the peace of God, which surpasses all understanding, will guard your hearts and your minds in Christ Jesus.*"

By bringing our feelings and concerns before God, we invite His peace to calm our turbulent hearts and minds. Furthermore, meditating on Scripture helps align our feelings with divine truths.

Seeking External Perspectives

Sometimes, when immersed in our feelings, gaining an external perspective can be invaluable. This might involve speaking to trusted individuals who can provide insights, comfort, or simply a listening ear. Whether it's friends, family, mentors, or professional counselors, others can often offer viewpoints that help us see beyond the immediacy of our feelings.

Developing Emotional Intelligence

Understanding and managing our emotions, a skill known as emotional intelligence, is vital. It involves recognizing our emotions, discerning their origins, and navigating them effectively. By developing emotional intelligence, teens can better handle emotional ups and downs, ensuring feelings don't control their actions or decisions.

In Conclusion

Emotions are a natural and essential part of our human experience. They add depth, color, and richness to life. However, they do not have to be the sole dictators of our actions or perceptions. With understanding, intentional reflection, and seeking God's wisdom, teens can navigate their feelings without being overwhelmed by them. Remember, you are not defined solely by how you feel in a fleeting moment.

REASON 5 Because Others Do Not Define Who You Are or Who You Will Be

In the vast tapestry of life, interwoven with relationships, interactions, and social constructs, there's a thread that stands out distinctly – the identity of an individual. Teens, especially, are on a journey of self-discovery, trying to understand who they are and where they fit in the world. Amidst this quest, it's easy to allow others—peers, teachers, family, and even society at large—to influence or dictate one's sense of self. Yet, an essential truth remains: *others do not, and should not, define who you are or who you will be.*

Understanding True Identity

Before diving into the complexities of external influences, it's pivotal to have a foundational understanding of identity from a biblical perspective.

Genesis 1:27 states, "*So God created man in his own image, in the image of God he created him; male and female he created them.*" Every individual is created in the image and likeness of God, which bestows inherent value, purpose, and a unique identity. Your worth is not contingent upon societal standards, popularity metrics, or external validations. It is rooted in the divine.

The Pressure of Conformity

Teen years often bring the challenge of navigating peer pressure and societal expectations. The desire to belong and be accepted can sometimes lead to conformity, even if it means compromising one's beliefs, values, or authentic self.

Romans 12:2 advises, "*Do not be conformed to this world, but be transformed by the renewal of your mind, that by testing you may discern what is the will of God, what is good and acceptable and perfect.*" This verse highlights the importance of not molding oneself according to worldly standards but seeking transformation and clarity through God's word.

The Weight of Labels and Stereotypes

Labels and stereotypes can confine and restrict individuals. Whether it's being categorized by academic prowess, physical appearance, socioeconomic background, or any other metric, these labels can create false limitations.

Yet, in Christ, these labels lose their power. Galatians 3:28 reminds us, "*There is neither Jew nor Greek, there is neither slave nor free, there is no male and female, for you are all one in Christ Jesus.*" Your identity in Christ transcends societal labels, offering freedom and authenticity.

Constructive Criticism vs. Detrimental Commentary

While constructive criticism can aid growth and development, not all feedback from others is beneficial. Detrimental commentary, which often stems from others' insecurities or prejudices, can erode self-worth if internalized.

It's crucial to develop discernment, differentiating between feedback that helps you grow and mere negativity. Remember, no individual has the authority or insight to define your entire being based on limited interactions or perspectives.

God's Perspective: The Only True Mirror

One of the most transformative realizations is seeing oneself through God's eyes. Psalm 139:13-14 reflects, "*For you formed my inward parts; you knitted me together in my mother's womb. I praise you, for I am fearfully and wonderfully made.*"

God knows you intimately—your strengths, weaknesses, dreams, fears—and He cherishes you. His perspective provides the most accurate reflection, free from the distortions of societal mirrors.

Your Future: A Blank Canvas

Your future remains a canvas waiting to be painted. Past mistakes, failures, or external labels don't dictate the masterpiece that can be created. With God as the guiding hand, there's potential for beauty, purpose, and impact beyond imagination.

Jeremiah 29:11 assures, "*For I know the plans I have for you, declares the LORD, plans for welfare and not for evil, to give you a future and a hope.*" This future is not constrained by others' expectations or definitions but is orchestrated by a loving God.

Empowering Personal Choice

While external influences are aplenty, every individual holds the powerful tool of choice. You can choose to seek validation from God rather than peers, to prioritize personal convictions over popularity, and to embrace the unique identity God has bestowed upon you.

In Conclusion

In the cacophony of voices trying to define, label, or influence, there's a steadfast truth that every teen should hold onto: *Your identity and destiny are divinely crafted, and no external voice holds the authority to alter that.*

Embrace your God-given identity, challenge the world's definitions, and walk in the freedom of knowing that others do not define who you are or who you will be. Your journey is uniquely yours, orchestrated by a loving Creator, filled with potential and purpose beyond measure.

REASON 6 Because Death Does Not Get Revenge on Those Who Hurt You

One of the profound misinterpretations of life's pains and betrayals, especially amidst the vulnerable years of adolescence, is the belief that ending one's life could serve as an ultimate act of revenge against those who have caused pain. However, this perspective, deeply rooted in hurt and misunderstanding, fails to recognize the broader scope of life, relationships, consequences, and the divine plan. Tragically, instead of vengeance, such an act often amplifies pain, regret, and confusion, impacting not just those who might have inflicted hurt but countless others as well.

Misunderstanding Revenge

At its core, the desire for revenge stems from a yearning for justice. When someone has been wronged or hurt, it's natural to want the perpetrator to feel a similar pain or regret. However, the belief that one's death can serve as a form of punishment or revenge is founded on two misunderstandings:

1. That it will primarily hurt the wrongdoer.
2. That it will bring satisfaction or justice to the one ending their life.

Yet, in reality, the aftermath of such a decision is a wave of compounded grief, affecting loved ones, acquaintances, and even those not directly connected.

The Ripple Effect of Grief

Death, especially when unexpected and self-inflicted, sends shockwaves through a community. Parents, siblings, friends, teachers, church members, and others are left grappling with guilt, sorrow, confusion, and a plethora of unanswered questions. Instead of directing pain towards a particular person, it spreads pain indiscriminately.

Proverbs 18:21 states, "*Death and life are in the power of the tongue,*" highlighting the profound impact our choices, even those made in silence, have on those around us. By misunderstanding revenge, a person might unintentionally bring pain upon those they never intended to hurt.

God's Perspective on Vengeance

From a biblical viewpoint, vengeance is not ours to dispense. Romans 12:19 advises, "*Beloved, never avenge yourselves, but leave it to the wrath of God, for it is written, 'Vengeance is mine, I will repay, says the Lord.'*" God, in His infinite wisdom and justice, understands the intricacies of every situation. By seeking personal vengeance, especially through irreversible acts, we bypass God's perfect plan for justice and redemption.

Seeking Healing Instead of Revenge

In the face of betrayal or pain, the healthier and more constructive path is seeking healing and forgiveness. While this might seem like an insurmountable challenge in the face of deep wounds, it's a journey worth undertaking.

1. **Therapeutic Intervention:** Engaging in professional counseling or therapy provides a safe space to process feelings of hurt, betrayal, and the desire for revenge. Counselors can offer coping strategies, perspectives, and tools to heal.
2. **Spiritual Support:** Engaging with spiritual leaders, mentors, or trusted members of the church can provide a spiritual perspective on hurt, forgiveness, and the path forward. Prayer, meditation on Scriptures, and engagement in Christian community can offer comfort and guidance.
3. **Forgiveness:** While it's a challenging step, forgiveness is a powerful tool for personal liberation. Ephesians 4:31-32 encourages, "*Let all bitterness and wrath and anger and clamor and slander be put away from you, along with all malice. Be kind to one another, tenderhearted, forgiving one another, as God in Christ forgave you.*" This isn't about condoning wrong actions but releasing the chains of bitterness and seeking personal peace.

Life's Potential for Restoration

While present circumstances might seem unbearable, life holds the potential for change, restoration, and redemption. Relationships can be mended, wrongs can be righted, and new beginnings are always possible.

Joel 2:25 promises, "*I will restore to you the years that the swarming locust has eaten,*" underscoring God's power to bring restoration in the face of devastation.

In Conclusion

The belief that death can serve as revenge is a heartbreaking misconception that amplifies pain rather than alleviating it. Every life, including those who have been deeply hurt, holds inherent value, potential, and purpose in God's grand tapestry. Seeking healing, understanding God's perspective on vengeance, and recognizing the profound ripple effects of our choices can guide individuals away from destructive paths. Remember, while pain is real, so is hope, redemption, and the promise of a better tomorrow.

REASON 7 Because Your Pain Is Not Permanent

Pain, in its multifaceted forms, can be one of the most overwhelming experiences in life. It can consume thoughts, overshadow joys, and even distort reality. Especially during the tumultuous years of adolescence, when every emotion is heightened, pain—whether emotional, physical, or spiritual—can feel unending. But a resounding truth that time and Scripture affirm is this: *your pain is not permanent.*

The Transitory Nature of Pain

Throughout life, everyone, irrespective of age or circumstance, will encounter periods of pain and discomfort. However, much like the seasons of nature, life's seasons of suffering are transitory. They come and go, sometimes leaving scars, yes, but also leaving behind lessons, resilience, and deeper understandings.

Biblical Affirmation of Temporary Troubles

The Bible, in its raw and unfiltered portrayal of human experiences, doesn't shy away from discussing pain. Yet, it consistently underlines the temporary nature of our earthly trials.

Paul, who was no stranger to suffering, remarked in 2 Corinthians 4:17, "*For this light momentary affliction is preparing for us an eternal weight of glory beyond all comparison.*" Paul's perspective reveals two essential truths: the troubles we face are light and momentary in the context of eternity, and they serve a purpose in God's grand design.

Growth Through Pain

While pain is undeniably challenging, it also has the potential to be a catalyst for growth. It's often in our most challenging times that we develop resilience, empathy, patience, and a deeper relationship with God.

James 1:2-4 encourages, "*Count it all joy, my brothers, when you meet trials of various kinds, for you know that the testing of your faith produces steadfastness. And let steadfastness have its full effect, that you may be perfect and complete, lacking in nothing.*" This isn't a call to be joyful about pain itself but to recognize the growth that can emerge from enduring it.

God's Comfort in the Midst of Pain

In the heart of anguish, it's comforting to know that God is not distant or uncaring. Psalm 34:18 assures, "*The Lord is near to the brokenhearted and saves the crushed in spirit.*" God's presence offers solace, understanding, and strength to endure. He doesn't promise a life devoid of pain, but He guarantees His unwavering presence throughout.

The Role of Community in Alleviating Pain

We weren't designed to go through life's trials in isolation. Christian community plays a pivotal role in providing support during painful periods. Sharing burdens, seeking counsel, and collective prayer are powerful tools in the healing process.

Galatians 6:2 instructs, "*Bear one another's burdens, and so fulfill the law of Christ.*" By leaning on and being there for one another, pain becomes more bearable, and healing accelerates.

Seeking Help When Pain Feels Overwhelming

It's crucial to understand that seeking help is not a sign of weakness. When pain feels insurmountable, reaching out for professional counseling or therapeutic intervention can be a lifeline. A trained perspective can offer coping strategies, a deeper understanding of the pain's roots, and pathways toward healing.

Tomorrow's Promise

While today might be marred by pain, tomorrow holds the promise of healing, joy, and new beginnings. Lamentations 3:22-23 beautifully captures this with the words, "*The steadfast love of the Lord never ceases; his mercies never come to an end; they are new every morning; great is your faithfulness.*" Every sunrise brings with it renewed hope and the potential for a better day.

In Conclusion

Pain, though a challenging facet of life, is not a life sentence. With time, support, faith, and the right interventions, the clouds of anguish can give way to clear skies of peace and joy. The journey through pain can lead to

THIRTEEN REASONS WHY YOU SHOULD KEEP LIVING

a deeper relationship with God, personal growth, and a more profound appreciation for life's joys.

For every teen experiencing the weight of pain, the message is clear: hold on, lean on your faith, and seek the support you need. *Because your pain is not permanent,* there's a hope-filled future awaiting you, filled with promise, purpose, and unparalleled joy.

Edward D. Andrews

REASON 8 Because you Can Control Your Life

In the whirlwind of adolescence, with its emotional peaks and valleys, pressures from society, and evolving sense of identity, it can often feel like life is a chaotic storm that's hard to navigate. Many teens might feel that they're merely reacting to external factors, perpetually influenced by events and people around them. However, there's a transformative realization that can change the trajectory of a young person's life: *you have control over your life.*

The Illusion of Helplessness

Many external factors can make teens feel helpless: academic pressures, peer dynamics, family issues, societal expectations, and more. This sense of helplessness, where one feels like a boat adrift in the sea without a rudder, can lead to feelings of despair.

However, this perception is just that—a perception. While you cannot control every event or how others behave, you can control your reactions, decisions, and actions.

God's Gift of Free Will

One of the unique gifts that God has given humanity is free will—the ability to choose. This gift, while profound, comes with responsibility. Deuteronomy 30:19 states, "*I have set before you life and death, blessing and curse. Therefore choose life, that you and your offspring may live.*" This Scripture emphasizes the importance and consequences of our choices. Each decision, no matter how small, can shape the course of your life.

Proactive Living: The Driver's Seat Approach

Instead of being mere passengers in their own lives, teens can take a proactive approach, steering their lives in the direction they desire.

1. **Set Clear Goals:** Understanding what you want in various areas—academic, spiritual, personal—can provide direction. It's like having a destination in mind before setting out on a journey.
2. **Decision-Making:** Every choice has consequences. By pausing to reflect on potential outcomes and seeking counsel when needed, you can make informed decisions that align with your goals and values.
3. **Embrace Responsibility:** Taking responsibility for one's actions, both good and bad, is empowering. It helps in learning from mistakes and celebrating successes.

The Power of Perspective

How you perceive challenges, setbacks, or even successes greatly influences your emotional and mental state. By adopting a positive, solution-oriented perspective, obstacles become opportunities for growth, and failures become lessons.

Romans 8:28 reminds us, "*And we know that in all things God works for the good of those who love him, who have been called according to his purpose."* This verse emphasizes that even in challenging circumstances, there's a divine plan at work, and with the right perspective, you can align with that plan.

Seeking Guidance and Wisdom

While it's empowering to know you have control over your life, it doesn't mean you have to navigate everything alone. Seeking guidance, whether from trusted adults, spiritual leaders, or God Himself, can provide clarity. Proverbs 3:5-6 advises, "*Trust in the LORD with all your heart and lean not on your own understanding; in all your ways submit to him, and he will make your paths straight.*"

Boundaries: The Art of Saying 'No'

Part of taking control of your life involves setting boundaries. This means recognizing what's healthy and beneficial for you and having the courage to say 'no' to situations or relationships that are detrimental.

In Conclusion

Life, especially during the adolescent years, can feel overwhelming. The cacophony of voices telling teens who to be, what to do, and how to feel can be deafening. Yet, amidst this noise, there's a powerful, liberating truth: *you can control your life.*

By understanding the gift of free will, adopting a proactive approach, seeking guidance, and setting boundaries, teens can navigate life's challenges with confidence and purpose. While storms will come, they're not helpless vessels but captains of their ships, with the power to choose their direction.

Every teen should remember: your life is a precious gift, filled with potential and purpose. Don't relinquish control to external pressures or fleeting emotions. Take charge, make informed decisions, and steer your life toward the bright future God has prepared for you.

Edward D. Andrews

REASON 9 Because Mental Difficulties Can Be Controlled and Overcome

The intricacies of the human mind are profound, shaping our emotions, behaviors, perceptions, and interactions. Especially during adolescence, when significant physical, emotional, and neurological changes are occurring, mental difficulties can emerge. These challenges, while real and sometimes daunting, come with an encouraging truth: *mental difficulties can be controlled and often overcome.*

Understanding Mental Difficulties

Before delving into avenues of control and healing, it's essential to have a grasp on what mental difficulties entail.

1. **Chemical Imbalances:** The brain's chemistry plays a significant role in mood and behavior. Imbalances in neurotransmitters, like serotonin or dopamine, can contribute to disorders such as depression or anxiety.

2. **Traumatic Events:** Experiencing or witnessing traumatic events can lead to post-traumatic stress disorder (PTSD) or other anxiety disorders.

3. **Genetics and Family History:** Some individuals might be predisposed to certain mental health

conditions due to their genetic makeup or family history.

4. **Life Pressures:** Challenges like academic stress, relationship problems, or bullying can result in anxiety, depressive episodes, or other mental difficulties.

God's View on Suffering

The Bible doesn't shy away from discussing suffering, including mental and emotional distress. Individuals like Elijah, David, and even Jesus experienced intense emotional moments. Yet, Scripture consistently points to hope, healing, and the compassionate nature of God.

Psalm 34:17-18 reads, "*When the righteous cry for help, the LORD hears and delivers them out of all their troubles. The LORD is near to the brokenhearted and saves the crushed in spirit.*" God's closeness and care are unwavering, especially during times of mental distress.

Professional Intervention: A God-Given Resource

One of the most beneficial steps for those facing mental difficulties is seeking professional intervention. Whether through therapy, counseling, or, when appropriate, medication, these avenues can provide relief, understanding, and coping mechanisms.

God has equipped medical professionals with knowledge and tools to assist in healing, much like He has gifted surgeons to mend physical ailments. Using these resources is not a sign of weak faith but rather a proactive step in seeking healing.

The Role of Community

In facing mental challenges, isolation can exacerbate symptoms. Engaging in a supportive community—be it through church, support groups, or trusted friend circles—can provide encouragement, understanding, and prayerful support.

Galatians 6:2 emphasizes the role of community, stating, "*Bear one another's burdens, and so fulfill the law of Christ.*" By sharing struggles and seeking support, the weight of mental difficulties can be lightened.

Personal Tools for Coping

Beyond external interventions, individuals can adopt personal practices to manage and overcome mental challenges:

1. **Routine:** Establishing a daily routine can provide a sense of normalcy and purpose.//
2. **Physical Activity:** Exercise can help regulate mood and alleviate symptoms of anxiety and depression.
3. **Healthy Diet:** What we consume can impact our brain chemistry. A balanced diet can support mental well-being.
4. **Limiting Stimulants:** Reducing or eliminating the intake of caffeine, nicotine, or certain medications can help manage anxiety symptoms.
5. **Spiritual Practices:** Engaging in prayer, meditation, and Scripture reading can offer comfort and perspective.

Embracing Hope and Resilience

While the journey through mental difficulties can be challenging, it's essential to embrace hope and resilience. Many individuals, with the right interventions and supports, have not only managed but have also overcome significant mental challenges, leading fulfilling lives.

2 Corinthians 4:16-18 encourages, "*So we do not lose heart. Though our outer self is wasting away, our inner self is being renewed day by day. For this light momentary affliction is preparing for us an eternal weight of glory beyond all comparison.*"

Edward D. Andrews

REASON 10 Because Loneliness is But Momentary

In the echoing chambers of loneliness, minutes can feel like hours and days can seem like years. Adolescence, a time marked by self-discovery and the desire for acceptance, can sometimes amplify feelings of isolation, leading many teens to believe they are fundamentally alone. However, the profound truth—one that can reshape perceptions and provide comfort—is this: *loneliness is but momentary.*

The Nature of Loneliness

Loneliness is not merely the physical absence of others but a deep-seated emotional and sometimes spiritual experience. It's the feeling that one is not understood, valued, or connected, even if surrounded by people.

1. **Transitional Phases:** Adolescence is a period of transitions—transitioning schools, friendship groups, even homes. These changes can result in temporary feelings of disconnection.

2. **Perceived Differences:** Feeling different or out-of-place, whether due to personal beliefs, interests, or experiences, can contribute to feelings of loneliness.

3. **Digital Disconnection:** In an age of digital connectivity, genuine interpersonal connections can sometimes be sparse, leading to a unique kind of digital-age loneliness.

Biblical Perspectives on Loneliness

Throughout Scripture, various figures have expressed feelings of isolation and desolation. Yet, even in their loneliest moments, they found solace in God's presence.

1. **David:** The Psalms are replete with David's raw emotions, including feelings of loneliness. Yet, he always turned to God in his despair. Psalm 62:1-2 reads, *"Truly my soul finds rest in God; my salvation comes from him. Truly he is my rock and my salvation; he is my fortress, I will never be shaken."*
2. **Elijah:** After a significant victory against the prophets of Baal, Elijah felt so alone and desolate that he wished for death. Yet, God met him in his loneliness, providing comfort and direction (1 Kings 19).
3. **Jesus:** In His earthly ministry, Jesus experienced profound loneliness, especially as He approached the cross. He cried out in the Garden of Gethsemane, deeply feeling the weight of impending separation from the Father. Yet, His story doesn't end in isolation but in triumphant resurrection and eternal connection.

Overcoming Loneliness: Practical Steps

1. **Seek Community:** Engaging in group activities, joining clubs or organizations, or becoming involved in church groups can help alleviate feelings of isolation. Shared experiences can foster genuine connections.

2. **Professional Counseling:** Therapists and counselors can provide tools and strategies to address feelings of loneliness, helping individuals build social skills and improve self-esteem.
3. **Limit Digital Consumption:** Reducing time on social media and focusing on face-to-face interactions can help combat digital-age loneliness.
4. **Volunteer:** Serving others can provide a dual benefit—alleviating feelings of isolation and providing a sense of purpose.
5. **Adopt a Pet:** For some, the companionship of an animal can provide comfort and reduce feelings of loneliness.

God's Everlasting Presence

For believers, the comforting truth is that they are never truly alone. Deuteronomy 31:8 promises, "*It is the Lord who goes before you. He will be with you; he will not leave you or forsake you. Do not fear or be dismayed.*" This divine companionship is unyielding, offering solace even in the loneliest moments.

The Transient Nature of Feelings

Feelings, including loneliness, are transient by nature. They come and go, influenced by circumstances, environments, and even physical health. Recognizing the temporary nature of loneliness can provide hope during challenging moments.

In Conclusion

While loneliness can cast a long shadow, obscuring the vibrant colors of life, it's essential to remember that it is a momentary experience. With proactive steps, divine assurance, and the understanding that feelings are fleeting, loneliness can be navigated and overcome.

To every teen wrestling with the weight of loneliness, remember: you are valued, understood, and never truly alone. *Because loneliness is but momentary,* brighter days of connection, community, and companionship await just over the horizon.

Edward D. Andrews

REASON 11 Because Substance Abuse Can Be Overcome

Substance abuse, which often begins as a way to escape pain, distress, or peer pressure, can quickly spiral into a relentless cycle of dependence and despair. Many teens, ensnared in this vicious trap, may feel an overwhelming sense of hopelessness, fearing they've ventured too far down a path of self-destruction. However, there exists a profound, life-altering truth: *substance abuse can be overcome.*

The Lure of Substance Abuse

Before understanding the path to recovery, it's crucial to acknowledge the factors that often lead teens to substance abuse:

1. **Peer Pressure:** The desire to fit in or be accepted can push many to try drugs or alcohol.
2. **Emotional Pain:** To numb emotional trauma, stress, or anxiety, some turn to substances as a temporary escape.
3. **Curiosity:** The natural adolescent curiosity might lead some to experiment, thinking they're immune to addiction.

Biblical Wisdom on Substance Use

The Bible, while not explicitly addressing modern drug abuse, provides timeless principles on temperance, self-control, and the dangers of intoxication. Proverbs 20:1 warns, "*Wine is a mocker, strong drink is raging: and whosoever is deceived thereby is not wise.*" This underscores the dangers of losing control and the deceptions of intoxication.

The Physical, Emotional, and Spiritual Consequences

Substance abuse isn't merely a physical concern. It affects the entirety of a person:

1. **Physical Impacts:** Drugs and alcohol can wreak havoc on the body, affecting vital organs, altering brain chemistry, and even leading to overdose or death.
2. **Emotional Toll:** Substance abuse can exacerbate feelings of depression, anxiety, and paranoia.
3. **Spiritual Consequences:** Dependence on substances can create a barrier between individuals and their relationship with God, leading to spiritual emptiness.

Hope in Overcoming: The Path to Recovery

While the challenges of substance abuse are undeniable, there's a beacon of hope. With the right resources, support systems, and determination, recovery is attainable.

1. **Acknowledgment:** The first step to recovery is acknowledging the problem. This self-awareness is crucial for seeking help.
2. **Professional Help:** Detoxification and rehabilitation centers offer structured environments for recovery, providing medical supervision, counseling, and therapies to address the root causes of addiction.
3. **Therapeutic Counseling:** A professional counselor can offer tools, coping mechanisms, and insights to prevent relapses and address the emotional triggers of substance abuse.
4. **Support Systems:** Recovery groups, such as Christian-based Alcoholics Anonymous or Celebrate Recovery, can provide peer support, accountability, and spiritual guidance.
5. **Rebuilding a Relationship with God:** Spiritual healing is a crucial aspect of holistic recovery. Engaging in prayer, Scripture meditation, and church community can renew one's relationship with God.

Prevention and Education

While recovery is possible, prevention is preferable. Educating teens about the dangers of substance abuse, offering them coping strategies for stress, and equipping them with refusal skills can be effective preventive measures.

Testimonies of Transformation

Countless individuals, once ensnared by the chains of addiction, have emerged victorious, testifying to the transformative power of faith, determination, and supportive intervention. Their stories serve as beacons of hope for others.

1 Corinthians 10:13 assures, "*No temptation has overtaken you except what is common to mankind. And God is faithful; he will not let you be tempted beyond what you can bear. But when you are tempted, he will also provide a way out so that you can endure it.*" This Scripture emphasizes that, with God's help, any challenge—including substance abuse—can be overcome.

In Conclusion

The shadow of substance abuse, dark and foreboding, does not signify an end but rather a challenging chapter in life's journey. With determination, support, and God's unwavering love, it's a chapter that can transition into a testimony of triumph and resilience.

To every teen battling the weight of addiction or tempted by the allure of substances, remember: *Because substance abuse can be overcome,* there's a brighter, hope-filled future awaiting you—one of freedom, purpose, and renewed joy.

Edward D. Andrews

REASON 12 Because Bullying and Cyberbullying Can Be Prevented

Facing Bullies: James' Story

One morning, Tom threatened James, saying, "If you come to school tomorrow, I'll hurt you bad." The next day, despite immense fear that made him physically sick, James went to school. Such traumatic events, varying in intensity, occur daily. Over 3.2 million students face bullying each year. Shockingly, around 160,000 teens skip school daily due to bullying. In the digital age, cyberbullying is on the rise, with 52% of young people reporting such incidents.

Defining Bullying

Bullying isn't just about physical harm. It's an unwanted, aggressive behavior among kids, usually showing a power imbalance. It either recurs or has the potential to. The victim and the bully both can face long-term issues. Key elements defining bullying are:

- **Power Imbalance**: Bullies exploit their power to intimidate others. This power could be physical strength, knowledge of someone's secrets, or popularity.
- **Repetition**: It's either a recurring behavior or possesses the potential to recur.

- **Types of Actions**: Bullying can range from threats, rumors, verbal or physical attacks, to deliberate exclusion from a group.

Different Bullying Types

1. **Physical Bullies**: These bullies resort to violent behaviors like:
    - Hitting, kicking, pinching
    - Spitting, pushing, tripping
    - Damaging someone's belongings
    - Making rude gestures
2. **Verbal Bullies**: They employ negative words to dominate:
    - Teasing and name-calling
    - Making inappropriate remarks
    - Threatening harm
3. **Relationship Bullies**: They manipulate relationships to maintain dominance:
    - Spreading rumors
    - Aiming to embarrass and shame others
4. **Reactive Victims**: Some, after facing bullying, turn into bullies themselves. This isn't a justification, merely an observation.
5. **Cyberbullying**: Using technology to harass:
    - Sending mean emails or texts

- Posting hurtful content on social platforms
- Spreading online rumors
- Sharing non-consensual photos

6. **Social Isolation**: Excluding someone to hurt them:
   - Purposeful exclusion from activities or groups
   - Encouraging others to avoid someone
   - Spreading rumors
   - Publicly embarrassing someone

The Global Reach of Bullying

Bullying is not restricted to one region; it's a global issue. Boys, on average, face 11% bullying rates, with Austria reporting the highest at 21%. Girls generally report lower bullying rates. Addressing and understanding this problem is crucial to creating safer environments for children worldwide.

Understanding Bullying and How to Counteract It

Reasons Why People Bully

1. **Past Experience**: Some bully because they were victims at one point, thinking it might offer them a safety net in social situations.

2. **Poor Role Models**: If a child observes bullying at home, either between siblings or from parents, they might emulate that behavior.

3. **Insecurities**: Often, bullies seek to mask their feelings of inadequacy by dominating others.

4. **Desire for Power**: Some individuals bully because they crave control and power, targeting those who appear weaker.

5. **Seeking Popularity**: To fit in with a certain group or gain popularity, some resort to bullying as a misguided way to impress peers.

6. **Thrill-Seeking**: Some privileged individuals resort to bullying for a sense of excitement or to alleviate boredom.

7. **Targeting Differences**: Differences, whether in terms of height, race, religion, beliefs, or background, can unfortunately make someone a target for bullying.

Responding to Bullying

Understanding that bullying is temporary and often fades after high school can be a solace. If possible, ignoring a bully can be effective, as they often seek reactions. It's essential to discern between empty threats and genuine threats. Here are some pointers:

- **Non-Reaction**: If a bully doesn't get the reaction they desire, they may lose interest.

- **Avoid Revenge**: Seeking revenge might escalate the situation, making it harder to resolve.

- **Safe Paths**: Adjust your routes to avoid places where known bullies congregate.
- **Stay Calm**: Avoid making antagonistic comments that could incite the bully.
- **Be Observant**: If you witness bullying, even if you're not the victim, consider reporting it. Recording evidence discreetly can be valuable.

Self-Defense and Building Resilience

While it's vital to try non-confrontational methods first, there may be times when standing up becomes necessary. Building physical strength and staying fit can deter potential bullies. Also, learning self-defense techniques can be empowering. While the world might have changed from simpler times, having the tools to defend oneself is invaluable.

Many correctional officers, for instance, undergo Aikido training – a Japanese martial art – to handle aggressive inmates. Similarly, equipping children with self-defense skills can prepare them for unforeseen challenges. In an unpredictable world, it's always better to be prepared than caught off guard.

Empower Your Children Against Bullying

Proactive Parenting Measures

As parents, it's crucial to equip your child with the skills to handle bullies from an early age. It's unwise to assume, "It's not my child's concern." One impactful way is to ensure your child maintains a healthy diet and follows a regular exercise regime. Notably, bullies are less inclined to target children who are physically fit. Simple actions like instructing your child to maintain a good posture, make eye contact, and communicate assertively can alter the way they are perceived by their peers. It's essential to provide them with a realistic understanding of the world, rather than an idealized perspective. Preparing them for real-world scenarios is not just beneficial but a necessary act of love.

Training for Self-Assurance

Right upbringing can empower your child not only to face bullies but also to shield others from such adversities. For parents who want to ensure their child is always a step ahead, enrolling them in unarmed self-defense classes can be invaluable. Even a couple of years of wrestling during grade school can equip a child to hold their own against larger opponents. Integrating disciplines like Aikido, wrestling, and basic boxing can enhance your child's physical fitness and, if ever required, could be life-saving.

REASON 13 Because Sexual Abuse Need Not Be a Lifetime of Pain

Sexual abuse is a harrowing violation, leaving deep scars in the hearts and minds of survivors. The aftermath of such a traumatic event can encompass a range of emotions, including shame, anger, fear, and intense pain. Many survivors grapple with the question, "Will this pain ever end?" The profound and hopeful answer is this: *Sexual abuse need not be a lifetime of pain.*

Understanding the Profound Impact of Sexual Abuse

Sexual abuse is a grievous breach of trust, violating one's sense of safety, dignity, and autonomy. For many survivors, especially if the abuse occurred during their formative years, its effects can manifest in various ways:

1. **Emotional Turmoil:** Feelings of guilt, shame, worthlessness, and self-blame are common among survivors.

2. **Physical Repercussions:** Some survivors may experience health issues, sleep disturbances, or somatic symptoms tied to the traumatic event.

3. **Relational Challenges:** Trusting others, especially in intimate relationships, can become profoundly challenging.

Biblical Insights on Pain and Healing

While the Bible does not shy away from discussing the reality of injustice and pain, it resoundingly emphasizes God's love, compassion, and promise of restoration. Victims of abuse can find solace in Scriptures that affirm their worth and the possibility of healing.

Psalm 34:18 assures, "*Jehovah is close to the brokenhearted and saves those who are crushed in spirit.*" This promise is a testament to God's unwavering presence during the darkest times.

Journey to Healing: Navigating the Aftermath

1. **Acknowledgment:** Recognizing and admitting the trauma is the first step towards healing. It's essential to understand that what happened was not the victim's fault.

2. **Professional Counseling:** Trauma-informed therapists can provide survivors with coping strategies, helping them process their emotions and eventually find closure.

3. **Support Groups:** Engaging in groups specifically designed for sexual abuse survivors can offer a safe space to share, relate, and heal collectively.

4. **Embracing the Healing Power of Faith:** A deep relationship with God can be a source of immense comfort. Prayer, meditation, and Scripture study can offer solace, strength, and a sense of purpose.

5. **Establishing Boundaries:** As survivors journey towards healing, establishing clear relational and personal boundaries can help regain a sense of control and safety.

The Role of the Christian Community

The Church can play a pivotal role in supporting survivors:

1. **Creating a Safe Space:** Churches should be sanctuaries where survivors feel safe, understood, and valued.
2. **Education:** Educating congregations about the reality and impact of sexual abuse can foster understanding and empathy.
3. **Offering Support:** Providing resources, counseling referrals, and support groups can significantly assist survivors in their healing journey.

A Future Beyond the Pain

While the scars of sexual abuse may remain, they need not dictate a survivor's future. With time, support, and faith, those scars can transform into symbols of resilience, strength, and hope.

Jeremiah 29:11 offers a promise that can resonate deeply with survivors, "*For I know the plans I have for you,*" *declares Jehovah, "plans to prosper you and not to harm you, plans to give you hope and a future.*"

In Conclusion

The pain and trauma of sexual abuse, while undeniably deep, need not be a life sentence of suffering. Through the combined power of faith, professional support, community, and inner resilience, survivors can chart a course towards a future marked by hope, healing, and renewed joy. To every teen survivor grappling with the weight of their past, remember: *Because sexual abuse need not be a lifetime of pain,* there's a brighter future awaiting you.

CHALLENGED SOULS 1
How Can I Overcome My Depression?

Depression is a term often thrown around casually, but it is a severe mental health condition that can grip individuals, altering their perception, feelings, and daily functioning. In the formative years of 12-25, many factors like hormonal changes, societal pressures, academic expectations, and personal relationships can exacerbate feelings of sadness, leading to depression. As a young Christian, it's essential to understand that while faith provides solace and strength, addressing depression often requires a multifaceted approach.

Understanding Depression

Symptoms: Depression is more than just feeling sad. It manifests in various ways, including:

- Persistent feelings of sadness, hopelessness, or emptiness
- Loss of interest in activities previously enjoyed
- Fatigue or decreased energy
- Difficulty concentrating, remembering, or making decisions
- Changes in appetite or unintended weight changes
- Sleep disturbances

- Thoughts of death or suicide

Causes: Depression can arise from a combination of genetic, biological, environmental, and psychological factors. Events such as trauma, loss of a loved one, a difficult relationship, or any stressful situation can also trigger it.

A Christian Perspective: Depression doesn't imply a lack of faith. Many devout believers, including biblical figures like King David and the prophet Elijah, exhibited symptoms consistent with depression. Remember, having depression isn't a sign of spiritual failure.

Steps to Overcoming Depression

Acknowledge the Issue: The first step is acceptance. Denying or suppressing your feelings can lead to further emotional complications. Remember the words in Psalm 34:18, "Jehovah is near to the brokenhearted; He saves those crushed in spirit."

Seek Professional Help: There's no shame in seeking help. A therapist or counselor, especially one with a Christian background, can offer guidance, coping techniques, and even medication if deemed necessary.

Stay Connected: Isolation can intensify feelings of depression. Engage with your church community, join a support group, or simply talk to trusted friends and family. Share your feelings and let them offer comfort.

Dive into Scripture: Scripture is a source of hope and encouragement. Verses like Psalm 42:11, "Why are you cast down, O my soul?... Hope in God; for I shall again praise him, my salvation and my God," can offer solace.

Prayer: While prayer isn't a substitute for medical treatment, it's a powerful tool to combat feelings of despair. Regularly pouring out your heart to God can be therapeutic.

Establish a Routine: A consistent daily routine can provide structure and a sense of purpose. Whether it's daily Scripture reading, a walk, or simply tidying up, these activities can instill a sense of accomplishment.

Avoid Alcohol and Drugs: These might seem like quick fixes but can exacerbate depression and decrease the effectiveness of antidepressant medications.

Stay Active: Physical activity releases endorphins, which are natural mood lifters. You don't need to run a marathon, but regular walks, stretching, or any form of exercise can help.

Limit Stress: If possible, try relaxation techniques such as deep-breathing exercises, meditation, or journaling. Remember, it's okay to seek peace and prioritize self-care.

Set Boundaries: Avoid overcommitting or taking on too many responsibilities. It's crucial to recognize your limits and communicate them to others.

Refrain from Making Major Decisions: Depression can cloud judgment. If possible, delay major decisions until your mood improves or discuss them with trusted advisors or family.

Limit Negativity: Minimize exposure to negative influences and negative self-talk. Surround yourself with positive affirmations and people.

Consider Dietary Changes: Some evidence suggests that foods with omega-3 fatty acids (like salmon and tuna) and folic acid (like spinach and avocado) might help ease depression.

Remember, It's a Process: Overcoming depression isn't an overnight journey. Celebrate small victories and understand that there might be setbacks. Rely on your faith, knowing that "He gives power to the faint, and to him who has no might he increases strength" (Isaiah 40:29).

In the throes of depression, it might seem like the darkness won't lift. But, with the right tools, support, and spiritual guidance, the journey towards the light becomes more accessible. Embrace the love and strength that comes from God, lean on your support system, and remember: there's no shame in seeking help. Your journey might be challenging, but through perseverance, faith, and professional guidance, you can find the path to healing and peace.

Edward D. Andrews

CHALLENGED SOULS 2
How Can I Overcome My Anxiety?

Anxiety is a pervasive emotion, especially in the tumultuous years of adolescence and young adulthood. For young people between 12-25, this emotion can be heightened by myriad factors, from academic pressures to social dynamics, from personal relationships to future uncertainties. As a young Christian, understanding and managing anxiety becomes pivotal, especially when seeking to align one's life with God's word and purpose. Navigating anxiety is not about suppressing it but learning to cope, manage, and eventually thrive.

Understanding Anxiety

Defining Anxiety: Anxiety is more than just feeling nervous or worried. When these feelings persist, become overwhelming, and interfere with daily life, they might be indicative of an anxiety disorder.

Symptoms:

- Restlessness or feeling on edge
- Becoming easily fatigued
- Difficulty concentrating or mind going blank
- Irritability
- Muscle tension

- Sleep disturbances

Causes: Anxiety can be the result of a combination of factors, including genetics, brain chemistry, personality, and life events. For young individuals, external pressures such as academic stress, peer pressures, and societal expectations can exacerbate these feelings.

A Christian Perspective: It's important to recognize that experiencing anxiety does not indicate a lack of faith or trust in God. Even the Apostle Paul admitted to feeling anxious about the churches he planted (2 Corinthians 11:28). What's crucial is how you address and manage these feelings in light of your faith.

Strategies for Overcoming Anxiety

Acknowledge the Feeling: Avoiding or denying your anxiety can amplify it. Recognize it, accept it, and remember Philippians 4:6-7, "Do not be anxious about anything, but in every situation, by prayer and petition, with thanksgiving, present your requests to God. And the peace of God, which transcends all understanding, will guard your hearts and your minds in Christ Jesus."

Engage in Prayer and Meditation: Regularly communicate with God. Share your worries and seek His peace. Meditation on Scripture can also be calming, grounding you in eternal truths amidst transient anxieties.

Seek Professional Guidance: A therapist or counselor can provide cognitive-behavioral strategies to manage and reduce anxiety. Opting for a Christian counselor can also ensure that the guidance you receive aligns with your faith.

Limit Stimulants: Reduce or eliminate the consumption of caffeine and sugar, as these can trigger or worsen anxiety.

Stay Active: Engage in regular physical activity. Exercise can help reduce anxiety and improve mood by releasing endorphins, the body's natural painkillers and mood elevators.

Rest and Sleep: Ensure you're getting adequate sleep. Establishing a regular sleep pattern can significantly impact your mood and energy levels.

Stay Connected: Regular fellowship with believers can provide a spiritual and emotional support system. Sharing your struggles with a trusted friend or mentor can be liberating.

Limit Exposure to Stressors: If watching the news or certain activities increase your anxiety, limit your exposure. Instead, engage in activities that promote peace and calm.

Set Realistic Goals: Set achievable tasks for yourself and celebrate your accomplishments. Breaking tasks into manageable chunks can make them less daunting.

Stay Informed: Understanding what triggers your anxiety can help in managing it. Keeping a journal can help identify patterns and triggers.

Grounding Techniques: Techniques such as the "5-4-3-2-1" method, where you identify five things you can see, four you can touch, three you can hear, two you can smell, and one you can taste, can help center you in moments of heightened anxiety.

Focus on the Present: Jesus said in Matthew 6:34, "Therefore do not be anxious about tomorrow, for tomorrow will be anxious for itself. Sufficient for the day is its own trouble." It's a call to focus on the present and trust God with our future.

In the journey of life, anxiety can sometimes feel like a constant companion, especially in our fast-paced, expectation-laden world. But with the right coping mechanisms, rooted in faith and complemented by professional guidance, it is possible to navigate through it. The road might seem challenging, but always remember: You're not alone in this journey. God is with you every step of the way, offering His peace, which surpasses all understanding.

Edward D. Andrews

CHALLENGED SOULS 3
How Can I Cope with This Constant Sadness?

The experience of persistent sadness can feel isolating and overwhelming, especially for young people navigating the volatile emotions of adolescence and early adulthood. Such emotions can be deeply entrenched, influencing every facet of one's life. But even in the depths of despair, there's hope, strength, and guidance to be found, particularly through a Christian perspective that promises healing, love, and understanding.

Understanding Persistent Sadness

Defining the Emotion: While everyone feels sad or down from time to time, constant sadness, especially when it lasts for more than two weeks and affects daily functioning, can be indicative of a deeper issue, like depression.

Symptoms:

- Feelings of hopelessness or pessimism
- Loss of interest in hobbies or activities
- Fatigue or decreased energy
- Difficulty concentrating or making decisions
- Sleep disturbances

- Appetite or weight changes
- Thoughts of death or suicide

Possible Causes: The origins of persistent sadness can be multifaceted, encompassing genetic factors, chemical imbalances in the brain, trauma, loss, or significant life changes.

A Christian Perspective: Experiencing such emotions isn't indicative of a lack of faith or God's abandonment. Remember Psalm 34:18: "The Lord is near to the brokenhearted and saves the crushed in spirit." God walks beside us, especially during our darkest moments.

Pathways to Coping and Healing

Connect with God: Foster an intimate relationship with Him through prayer, Scripture, and worship. By leaning into God's promises and seeking His presence, one can find solace and hope.

Scriptural Comfort: Meditate on scriptures that address sadness and despair. For instance, Psalm 42:11 says, "Why, my soul, are you downcast? Why so disturbed within me? Put your hope in God, for I will yet praise him, my Savior and my God."

Seek Professional Help: It's crucial to consult with a therapist or counselor, especially when sadness hampers daily functioning. Christian counseling can be particularly helpful in providing spiritual and therapeutic solutions.

Engage in Community: Isolation can exacerbate feelings of sadness. Surrounding oneself with a loving community, like a church or support group, can offer encouragement and a sense of belonging.

Healthy Lifestyle Choices: Engage in regular physical activity, maintain a balanced diet, and get adequate rest. These can play a pivotal role in emotional well-being.

Set Small Goals: Breaking tasks into manageable steps and setting priorities can alleviate feelings of being overwhelmed. Celebrate small victories, for they contribute to a greater sense of accomplishment.

Limit Stress: If possible, avoid known stressors. Explore relaxation techniques such as deep breathing, meditation, and journaling to handle stress.

Limit Alcohol and Avoid Drugs: These can make sadness worse and decrease the efficacy of antidepressant medicines.

Avoid Making Important Decisions When Down: Your perspective is skewed when in the throes of deep sadness. Give yourself time and seek guidance before making significant decisions.

Establish Routine: Maintaining a routine can offer a feeling of normality. Even simple things like setting specific mealtimes or allocating time for reading can make a difference.

Limit Negativity: Reduce exposure to negative influences and negative self-talk. Surrounding oneself with positivity, whether it's in the form of uplifting music, books, or company, can influence mood.

Stay Connected: Even a brief chat with a loved one can make a difference. Share your feelings and concerns, letting others in can be healing.

Remember God's Love and Faithfulness: Despite feelings of despair, remember that God's love remains constant. Romans 8:38-39 assures us that nothing "will be able to separate us from the love of God that is in Christ Jesus our Lord."

For young Christians experiencing constant sadness, the journey can be harrowing. Yet, with faith, support, and appropriate interventions, there's a way forward. No darkness is so profound that it can quench the enduring light of God's love and promise. Seeking help, whether divine, professional, or communal, isn't a sign of weakness, but of strength and self-awareness. It's a testament to one's commitment to healing, growth, and a life that honors God.

Edward D. Andrews

CHALLENGED SOULS 4
Protecting Children from Woke Ideological Education: A Biblical Perspective

This chapter provides biblical and practical insights for parents concerned about woke ideological education infiltrating schools. From fostering open communication and biblical foundations to exploring alternative education options, learn how to safeguard your children's minds and hearts.

Worried about the influence of woke ideology in your children's education? Gain a biblical perspective on protecting your children from such indoctrination. This article offers practical steps, grounded in Scripture, to help parents vigilantly monitor and guide their children's educational experience.

In today's complex social climate, parents face unprecedented challenges in raising their children according to the timeless principles of Scripture. Among these challenges is the incursion of "woke" ideological education into the school system, pushing agendas like critical race theory, gender ideology, and various forms of liberalism. These teachings stand in stark contrast to a biblical worldview. Let's explore how Christian parents can navigate this tricky landscape to protect their children.

Know What Your Children Are Learning

Key Scripture: Proverbs 22:6

"Train up a child in the way he should go; even when he is old he will not depart from it."

Core Principle: Parents should be actively involved in what their children are being taught. They should not hesitate to scrutinize lesson plans, textbooks, and school communication.

Counter-Educate with Scriptural Principles

Key Scripture: Ephesians 6:4

"Fathers, do not provoke your children to anger, but bring them up in the discipline and instruction of the Lord."

Core Principle: Counteract any unbiblical teachings with a strong foundation of biblical principles at home. Make the Bible and its teachings a regular part of your family life.

Be Aware of Subtle Influences

Key Scripture: 2 Corinthians 11:14-15

"And no wonder, for even Satan disguises himself as an angel of light. So it is no surprise if his servants, also, disguise themselves as servants of righteousness."

Core Principle: The danger often lies not in overt teachings but in subtle insinuations and activities designed to manipulate children's perceptions of self and reality, like the case of Jenny mentioned in your scenario.

Engage with Teachers and School Officials

Key Scripture: Matthew 10:16

"Behold, I am sending you out as sheep in the midst of wolves, so be wise as serpents and innocent as doves."

Core Principle: Maintain an active relationship with the teachers and staff at your child's school. Politely but firmly express any concerns you have about the ideological content of the education they are providing.

Consider Alternative Education Options

Key Scripture: Romans 12:2

"Do not be conformed to this world, but be transformed by the renewal of your mind, that by testing you may discern what is the will of God, what is good and acceptable and perfect."

Core Principle: Depending on the severity of the ideological indoctrination, parents may need to consider alternative educational options such as homeschooling or Christian schools that align with biblical values.

Legal Recourse and Civil Disobedience

Key Scripture: Acts 5:29

"But Peter and the apostles answered, 'We must obey God rather than men.'"

Core Principle: As last resorts, legal action or even civil disobedience may be necessary to protect your children. In the given case of Jenny, the parents had every biblical and moral right to protect their child from a dangerous and life-altering ideology.

Emotional and Spiritual Support

Key Scripture: 1 Thessalonians 5:11

"Therefore encourage one another and build one another up, just as you are doing."

Core Principle: Even when you take all the right steps, your child may still be influenced by destructive ideologies. Provide a strong emotional and spiritual support system at home, grounded in the love and teachings of Christ.

The Bible offers wisdom for every situation, including the modern challenges posed by ideological education contrary to biblical principles. Parents need to be vigilant, proactive, and rooted in the Word of God to effectively shield their children from these harmful influences. In extreme cases, like that of Jenny, the consequences of inaction can be devastating, altering a child's life in unimaginable ways. Therefore, it is imperative that parents take this stewardship seriously, trusting in God for wisdom and guidance.

Edward D. Andrews

The Reckoning of Jennifer: A Journey from Jenny to Johnny and Back Again

The Genesis of Confusion

It was a bright September morning when five-year-old Jenny crossed the threshold of Mrs. Winterton's kindergarten class. Mrs. Winterton, a staunch advocate for progressive ideologies, noticed Jenny playing with toy trucks. This, in her mind, was the *opportunity*—to mold and guide, though some would say manipulate, a young soul into a narrative deeply disconnected from Jenny's Christian upbringing.

"Jenny," Mrs. Winterton leaned down and whispered, "have you ever felt like you're really a boy inside? Remember, this is our little secret."

Over the next six years, a concerted, cultish effort unfolded within the school to steer Jenny away from her God-given identity. Worksheets, discussions, and counseling sessions were strategically employed to imprint upon Jenny that she was born into the wrong body.

When Hormones Speak Louder Than Words

At the vulnerable age of 12, the school initiated hormone therapy for Jenny, now going by Johnny. This chemical intervention marked her body and psyche in irreversible ways. Her voice deepened; body hair sprouted where it had never been.

The school finally decided to inform Jenny's parents—staunch, God-fearing Christians—of the "transformation."

"Jenny is now Johnny, and he's been undergoing hormone therapy for a while now," announced the principal. "We're also preparing for gender-reassignment surgery in two years."

Faith Versus System

"Absolutely not," Jenny's mother broke down in tears, clutching a Bible to her chest. "You are trying to destroy God's creation!"

"This is child abuse!" the father roared. "Jenny is a girl, created in the image of God!"

But their pleas fell on deaf ears. Labeling them as abusers, the school took them to court and won. Jenny was taken from her home and, at 14, underwent the irreversible surgery that detached her not just from her biological reality but also from her spiritual heritage.

Awakening

A decade passed. At 24, Jenny—living as Johnny—stumbled upon a Bible that had lain forgotten in her apartment. The words of Genesis leapt off the pages: "So God created man in his own image, in the image of God he created him; male and female he created them" (Genesis 1:27).

Her eyes swelled with tears. The years of ideological programming began to crumble. She realized she had been living a fabricated life, a distortion of the beautiful reality God had intended for her.

The Cost of Truth

Jenny's life turned into a cascade of psychiatric consultations and de-transition procedures. Yet, she was shattered to discover the irreversible havoc the hormone therapies had wrought—she would never bear children.

In a reckoning moment, Jenny took legal action against the school for grooming her into a life that robbed her of her most fundamental identity. After a tumultuous battle, the court ruled in her favor, awarding her three million dollars.

But what is the worth of three million dollars when your very essence has been stolen, manipulated, and destroyed?

Redeeming the Broken Pieces

Today, Jennifer lives a life of advocacy, warning parents and schools of the irreversible damage that ideological indoctrination can cause. While money can never replace what was stolen from her, her story serves as a cautionary tale—one of a life nearly ruined by a narrative that contradicted the fundamental biblical truths she had once held dear.

The words of Scripture that once comforted her family now provided her solace and a sense of mission: "Train up a child in the way he should go; even when he is old he will not depart from it" (Proverbs 22:6).

Though Jennifer cannot regain her lost years or her ability to bear children, she's found a renewed sense of purpose: to protect innocent lives from being ensnared by ideologies that defy God's beautiful design for human sexuality and identity.

The Inextinguishable Light

Jennifer found solace in her faith, finding her identity not in a cultural narrative but in her Creator. Her story, both heartbreaking and redeeming, serves as a stark reminder that when human designs conflict with Divine plans, the soul will inevitably yearn for the truth—a truth that can only be found in the sacred words of Scripture and the eternal love of God.

And so, Jennifer stands, a broken vessel, yet one that reflects the light of undeniable, Scriptural truth—a light that no amount of darkness can extinguish.

Preventative Measures for Protecting Children from Ideological Indoctrination

Open Communication Channels

First and foremost, parents must establish open lines of communication with their children. This means not merely talking *at* them but talking *with* them. "Train up a child in the way he should go; even when he is old he will not depart from it" (Proverbs 22:6). This training is a two-way street. Children should feel comfortable coming to their parents with any questions or concerns.

Vigilant Oversight of Educational Content

Parents should be vigilant in understanding what their children are being taught at school. This means reviewing textbooks, talking to teachers, and even sitting in classes if possible. If a curriculum is found to include elements contrary to biblical teachings, parents have a responsibility to take action—whether that means meeting with teachers, talking to administrators, or moving their child to a different educational setting.

Foster a Strong Biblical Foundation

Children should have a robust understanding of biblical principles from an early age. Daily family devotions, Scripture memorization, and candid discussions about biblical viewpoints on contemporary issues can lay a strong foundation. The Bible says, "These commandments that I give you today are to be on your hearts. Impress them on your children. Talk about them when you sit at home and when you walk along the road, when you lie down and when you get up" (Deuteronomy 6:6-7).

Teach Critical Thinking Skills

Teach your children not only *what* to think but *how* to think. This involves equipping them to assess an argument critically, to discern logical inconsistencies, and to identify manipulative tactics. Children who can think critically are less likely to be swept away by persuasive but flawed arguments.

Social Media and Peer Monitoring

Parents must be aware of not only what their children are being taught but also who they are associating with. Social media platforms are a hotbed for all kinds of ideologies. Ensure that your children understand the perils and pitfalls of using such platforms and monitor their usage.

Parental Involvement in School Activities

Being actively involved in school events and committees allows parents to be part of shaping the school environment. It also enables them to know what ideological issues may be infiltrating the school setting.

Legal Recourse and Rights

Know your rights as a parent. When you disagree with a teacher's or school's ideological stance that contradicts biblical truths, it's essential to understand the legal protections available to you. Engage with legal organizations committed to protecting religious freedom if you encounter challenges.

Strong Support Systems

Cultivate a strong support system composed of like-minded families, your church community, and possibly even legal experts who can offer advice. The saying, "It takes a village to raise a child," has a grain of truth. A strong, biblically-minded community can offer invaluable support in standing against ideological indoctrination.

Alternatives to Public Education

Consider alternative education options like homeschooling or Christian schools that align with your biblical beliefs. "Do not be yoked together with unbelievers. For what do righteousness and wickedness have in common? Or what fellowship can light have with darkness?" (2 Corinthians 6:14).

Being proactive, vigilant, and biblically grounded are the keys to safeguarding your children from destructive ideological influences. These measures are not guarantees, but they significantly reduce the risk of your children falling prey to harmful ideologies. Your home must become a sanctuary of biblical truth in a world increasingly hostile to such values. By fortifying this sanctuary, you're doing your God-given duty to protect and nurture the souls entrusted to your care.

The Exposure to Distorted Information on Sexual Matters at School

Today's educational landscape is fraught with pitfalls for young minds, especially when it comes to sexual education. Some schools, under the guise of being "progressive" or "inclusive," introduce sex education curriculums that promote ideologies contrary to Biblical principles. These can range from normalizing premarital sex to encouraging exploratory sexual behavior from an early age. Such distortions are often presented as "facts," leaving children confused and vulnerable. The Apostle Paul warned against such distortions, stating, "Let no one deceive you with empty words" (Ephesians 5:6).

Countering Sexual Misinformation

The best way to counteract sexual misinformation is through *clear, honest, and Biblical communication*. Parents should be the primary educators when it comes to sexual matters. By instilling a Biblical view of sexuality from a young age, children will be better equipped to discern falsehoods. Proverbs 22:6 says, "Train up a child in the way he should go; even when he is old he will not depart from it." Knowing the truth helps children recognize lies. Moreover, parents should stay informed about the curriculum taught at their child's school and, if necessary, seek alternative educational options that align with a Biblical worldview.

Biblical Insights on Sexual Matters

The Bible has much to say about sexual matters, presenting them within the context of marital commitment and mutual love. 1 Corinthians 7:2-3 advises, "But because of the temptation to sexual immorality, each man should have his own wife and each woman her own husband. The husband should give to his wife her conjugal rights, and likewise the wife to her husband." Hebrews 13:4 further emphasizes the sanctity of marital relations: "Let marriage be held in honor among all, and let the marriage bed be undefiled." The Bible clearly delineates sexual boundaries, emphasizing purity, fidelity, and the sacredness of the marriage covenant.

No Correlation Between Godly Knowledge and Immorality

Contrary to the notion that talking about sex will lead to sexual activity, *Biblically-grounded sexual education can serve as a protective measure.* When children understand the God-ordained purpose and boundaries of sexual relations, they are less likely to engage in immoral behavior. The Apostle Paul encouraged believers to "abstain from sexual immorality" and to "know how to control your own body in holiness and honor" (1 Thessalonians 4:3-4). Information grounded in God's Word serves to guide rather than tempt.

Progressive Education on Intimate Matters

Children should be taught about sexual matters progressively, in a manner appropriate to their age and level of understanding. Just as you wouldn't teach advanced calculus to a first-grader, there are appropriate times and ways to introduce various aspects of sexuality. The key is to be attentive and open, answering questions and providing guidance as the child matures. This can be likened to how Jesus tailored His teachings to His audience's level of spiritual maturity, stating in John 16:12, "I still have many things to say to you, but you cannot bear them now."

To conclude, we live in a world increasingly indifferent or even hostile to Biblical principles, especially regarding sexuality. It's imperative for parents to be vigilant, proactive, and grounded in the Word of God to guide their children effectively through the maze of sexual misinformation.

CHALLENGED SOULS 5
Help for Those Who Are Struggling with Transgender Ideology?

This chapter offers a range of questions and biblical counsel to help individuals grappling with transgender ideology. Discover how compassion and biblical truth can guide you back to God's intended design for your life as male or female.

In today's culture, issues surrounding transgender ideology have become increasingly complex and polarizing. The role of a Christian counselor is to approach these issues with both biblical fidelity and compassionate understanding. When counseling those struggling with transgender ideology, it's crucial to pose thoughtful questions that encourage self-examination while also providing biblical perspectives that offer clarity and hope.

Questions for Self-Examination

1. **Do you understand your intrinsic value as created by God?**

    - Scripture tells us that everyone is made in the image of God (Genesis 1:27). How does this biblical truth influence your understanding of your worth? [More on this below]

2. **What is your ultimate source of identity?**

- Are you seeking your identity in your gender or in Christ? According to the New Testament, our identity should be in Christ (Galatians 3:26-29).

3. **What fears or concerns do you have about conforming to biological gender norms?**

- What does it mean for you to be a man or a woman, and how does that align with or contradict God's design in Scripture?

4. **Have you considered the long-term implications?**

- Physical alterations like hormone therapy or surgeries have long-lasting consequences. Have you considered what God's Word says about our bodies being temples of the Holy Spirit (1 Corinthians 6:19-20)?

5. **Are you experiencing a form of suffering or distress?**

- Is this issue of transgender ideology linked to a particular form of suffering or distress in your life? How does Scripture guide us in dealing with suffering (Romans 5:3-5)?

6. **What are your beliefs about God's design for gender and sexuality?**

- Do your beliefs align with the biblical teaching that God created man and woman (Genesis 5:2), and that this creation has particular roles and functions (Ephesians 5:22-33)?

7. **How are you engaging with community?**

- Are you isolating yourself or are you seeking wisdom from a community that aligns with biblical principles? (Proverbs 11:14)

8. **Have you prayed about this struggle?**

- Prayer is our primary means of communication with God. Have you sought God's wisdom and guidance concerning these feelings (James 1:5)?

Biblical Counseling Perspectives

1. **Reaffirm Human Dignity**

- Regardless of their struggles, everyone is created in God's image and therefore possesses intrinsic value. Show them love and respect as Christ loved us. [More on this below]

2. **Root Identity in Christ**

- Encourage them to find their identity in Christ, not in gender. Highlight Scriptures that show our identity as children of God through faith in Christ (John 1:12; Galatians 3:26-29).

3. **Focus on God's Design**

- Remind them that God, as the Designer of all creation, designed the concept of male and female* with specific intentions (Genesis 1:27). Discomfort with one's biological sex is an indication that something is amiss, and the solution is not necessarily altering one's body but seeking alignment with God's design.

4. **Long-Term Implications**

- Discuss the long-lasting medical, emotional, and spiritual ramifications of transitioning. Instead, suggest that they focus on becoming the man or woman that God created them to be, embracing the biological sex He assigned them at birth.

5. **Engage with Community**
   - Encourage them to connect with a community that will support them in a biblical manner. This community could include pastors, mature Christian friends, or Christian counselors who can provide additional guidance.

6. **Commitment to Prayer**
   - Encourage consistent prayer for wisdom and for God's will to be done. Reiterate the importance of relying on God for understanding and guidance.

7. **Scripture for Encouragement**
   - Share Scriptures that speak to God's love, grace, and transforming power. Passages such as Romans 12:2 can be particularly comforting.

8. **No Instant Solutions**
   - Make it clear that neither you nor they have all the answers now and that it's a journey that will require ongoing reliance on God and His Word.

9. **Offer Hope**
   - Ultimately, the Gospel message is one of hope. Despite the struggles we face in this life, the hope of eternal life through Jesus Christ is always available to us.

It's crucial to guide those struggling with transgender ideology to the infallible truths found in Scripture while being sensitive to the emotional and psychological distress they may be experiencing. The objective is to offer biblical counsel that leads to genuine freedom in Christ.

Made In the Image of God

The foundational biblical teaching that humans are made in the image of God should not be misconstrued to suggest that God endorses or supports a departure from the biological categories of male and female* that He created. Scripture is clear on this matter: God made human beings male and female* (Genesis 1:27). There is no biblical support for the idea that a multitude of genders exists; rather, the binary nature of gender is affirmed consistently throughout Scripture.

Moreover, being made in the image of God is not an endorsement of our fallen desires or propensities. All humans have a proclivity toward sin, a point that is emphasized in Genesis 6:5 and 8:21, which state that human thoughts are inclined toward evil. Jeremiah 17:9 further drives home the idea that the human heart is inherently deceitful and wicked. So, if someone claims that their feelings toward the opposite gender are divinely ordained because they are made in God's image, that argument is not consistent with what Scripture teaches about our fallen nature.

Addressing the matter practically, we do indeed have a range of desires and inclinations that are out of step with God's design, such as the propensity for sexual addiction for some. However, the presence of these desires doesn't justify acting upon them. Instead, these are areas of our lives that require transformation and renewal, as you've rightly pointed out.

Paul's teachings offer substantial hope in this regard. We are endowed with a conscience that distinguishes right from wrong (Romans 2:14-15), and this moral compass needs to be cultivated and shaped by God's Word. A neglected or repeatedly violated conscience can grow "seared" or calloused (1 Timothy 4:2), no longer providing reliable moral guidance.

Paul strongly encourages believers to "put on the new self" (Ephesians 4:24; Colossians 3:10), which is the regenerated nature that aligns with God's will. We are also urged to adopt the mind of Christ (Philippians 2:5; 1 Corinthians 2:16; Romans 15:5), a transformation that comes through the renewing of our minds (Romans 12:2). As we immerse ourselves in Scripture and surround ourselves with godly influences, our thinking becomes increasingly aligned with God's will.

In the same vein, Paul also exhorts believers to gain control over their bodies, referred to as "vessels" in passages like 1 Thessalonians 4:4. This means exercising self-control, a fruit of the Spirit (Galatians 5:23), and ensuring our bodies are instruments for righteous acts and not sinful desires.

So, if someone is struggling with transgender ideology or other feelings contrary to God's design, the counsel remains the same: Work on renewing the mind and transforming the heart according to God's Word. Aligning oneself with God's designed order for gender is a part of the broader Christian call to live righteously and holistically, something achievable through the empowering grace of God and the renewing knowledge of His Word.

What is a Woman?

* In the current cultural conversation, the definitions of "woman," "sex," and "gender" have become points of contention. There is an increasing tendency to differentiate between "sex" and "gender," with the former being viewed as biological and the latter as a social construct subject to fluidity. While the categories of "sex" and "gender" are indeed recognized in various disciplines, it's crucial to address this subject from a biblical perspective to counter unbiblical and unbiological assertions.

According to Scripture, the terms "sex" and "gender" are not separate categories but are intrinsically connected. God created human beings as male and female, and this binary categorization is rooted in biology and affirmed in theology (Genesis 1:27; 5:2). There's no room in this biblical framework for a multitude of genders or for the separation of gender from one's biological sex. Consequently, being a "woman" is not a socially constructed role or a personal choice but is rooted in the design of God.

The Hebrew expression for "woman" is 'ish·shah', essentially meaning a "female man." This term can also be translated as "wife," reflecting the interrelatedness of roles and identity between men and women in both the family and broader societal structures. The Greek term gy·ne' holds a similar dual meaning, being translated both as "woman" and "wife." In both cases, the terms are relational but grounded in biology. They do not offer an abstract, socially constructed concept of womanhood that can be molded to fit individual preferences or societal changes.

Moreover, the attempt to decouple "gender" from biology on the grounds that gender roles and characteristics are "taught" does not align with the biblical teaching that male and female distinctions were designed by God and are part of the created order. While it's true that societies have norms and roles, these are not what fundamentally define men and women. In the biblical view, a woman is, by definition, an adult human female who has passed the age of puberty. Her identity as a woman is not a social construct but a biological and theological fact.

Indeed, gender roles, as described in Scripture, are relationally significant. They carry both equal worth and different responsibilities in the context of family and church life (Ephesians 5:22-33; 1 Timothy 2:11-15). However, these roles are not arbitrarily or culturally imposed but are derived from the created order.

Addressing the issue pastorally, those struggling with gender dysphoria or confusion should be approached with compassion, acknowledging the psychological and emotional complexities involved. Yet, compassion must be coupled with truth. It would not be truly loving to affirm someone in a self-perception that conflicts with their God-given biological and theological identity.

In summary, from a biblical perspective, a woman is an adult human female whose identity as a female is not a social construct but a divinely ordained reality. The current attempts to redefine or expand the categories of "sex" and "gender" are not compatible with biblical teaching. The challenge for the Church is to compassionately engage with those who experience confusion in this area while steadfastly upholding the truth of Scripture.

CHALLENGED SOULS 6
What Does the Bible Say About Transgenderism and Cross-Dressing?

Some have shied away from using Old Testament Bible verses to talk about how we are to live our Christian life. They might say, "but some things in the Old Covenant Law were only for Israel." Or they might say, "Christians are not under the Mosaic Law." This is somewhat true, Christians are not under the Mosaic Law, but God does not change when it comes to moral values. How he felt then is how he feels now. Christians are not obligated to keep the ceremonial aspect of the Mosaic Law, but they are obligated to live by the principles of the Old Testament.

For example, Deuteronomy 22:5 is a verse in the Bible that says, "A woman shall not wear a man's garment, nor shall a man put on a woman's cloak, for whoever does these things is an abomination to the Lord your God." This verse is not discussing *styles* of clothing. The prohibition is regarding one's wearing on things specifically designed for the opposite sex. This verse is often interpreted as a prohibition against cross-dressing or wearing clothing that is traditionally associated with the opposite gender. It is believed to be part of a larger set of rules and regulations that were given to the Israelites by God through Moses, and it is considered to be a part of God's moral code for the Israelites. The verse is often understood to be a command for men and women to adhere to traditional gender roles and to dress in a way that is appropriate for their gender. It is also seen as a way to prevent confusion and maintain social order within the community.

When it comes to appearance and clothing, generally, a man wants to look like a man, and a woman wishes to look like a woman. For God's servant, be it an Israelite or a Christian, to behave contrary to this deep God-given sense of what is fitting would displease God. When Deuteronomy was written in the late 15th century BCE, men and women wore robes. However, there was a distinction between the clothing of men and women. The principle here in Deuteronomy 22:5 would not rule out a woman's wearing pants.

And it is true that Christians are not under the Mosaic Law. (Rom. 6:14) Insistence on applying the written form of a law or rule rather than its spirit or intent would be in opposition to Christian teaching. So, women wearing pants today would not be in opposition to the law, which was to prevent confusion about sexual identity and sexual abuse. While Christians are not under the Mosaic law, they are guided by its principles, which means using discernment, good judgment, and applying their conscience. The Bible's counsel is that women "women should adorn themselves in respectable apparel, with modesty and self-control, . . . but with what is proper for women who profess godliness, with good works."—1 Tim. 2:9-10.

The Bible and Cross-Dressing and Transgenderism

The New Testament does not explicitly address the issue of cross-dressing or identifying oneself with words that denote members of the opposite sex or transgenderism.

However, there are a few passages in the New Testament that could be interpreted as addressing these issues.

For example, in Deuteronomy 22:5, it is written: "A woman must not wear men's clothing, nor a man wear women's clothing, for the Lord your God detests anyone who does this." This verse could be understood as prohibiting cross-dressing.

In addition, 1 Corinthians 6:9 lists "effeminate" (malakoi in Greek) and "homosexuals" (arsenokoitai in Greek) among those who will not inherit the kingdom of God. The two Greek terms refer to passive men partners and active men partners in consensual homosexual acts. "nor men of passive homosexual acts [μαλακοὶ], nor men of active homosexual acts [ἀρσενοκοῖται]"

It is possible to interpret the passage in 2 Peter 2:10, which speaks of those who "indulge in the lust of defiling passion and despise authority," as applying to certain aspects of transgenderism.

In this verse, the author is warning against certain people who are indulging in sinful behaviors and showing contempt for authority. These people are described as bold and willful, and they do not show fear or respect when they speak against those who are held in high regard. The phrase "the lust of defiling passion" likely refers to sexual immorality or other forms of impurity, and the phrase "the glorious ones" could refer to angels or other beings of high status. Overall, the verse is cautioning against following the example of those who engage in sinful behaviors and disrespect authority, as such behavior is seen as sinful and disrespectful in the context of the Bible.

PREPARING YOUR APOLOGETICS BY KNOWING WHAT THEY MIGHT SAY

The New Testament does not directly address the issue of transgenderism, as the concept of gender identity and the experience of being transgender were not understood in the same way in the cultural context in which the New Testament was written. However, there are a few passages in the New Testament that those who support transgenderism might interpret as addressing issues related to gender and identity.

For example, in Galatians 3:28, it is written: "There is neither Jew nor Gentile, neither slave nor free, nor is there male and female, for you are all one in Christ Jesus." This verse, they would argue, suggests that in Christ, distinctions of gender, social status, and ethnicity are not important and that all people are equal. They would argue that this message of equality and inclusion could potentially be applied to the issue of transgenderism. Galatians 3:28 is a verse in the epistle to the Galatians, a letter written by the apostle Paul to a group of early Christian churches in the region of Galatia. The verse reads: "There is neither Jew nor Greek, there is neither slave nor free, there is no male and female, for you are all one in Christ Jesus." In this verse, Paul is emphasizing the unity and equality of believers in Christ. He is saying that in Christ, there is no distinction based on ethnicity (Jew or Greek), social status (slave or free), or gender (male or female). Instead, all believers in Christ are united and considered equal. This message of unity and equality is a central theme in the epistle to the Galatians, as Paul was addressing issues of division and conflict within the Christian community in Galatia. Overall, the verse is an important reminder that in the eyes of God, all believers in Christ are equal and united in their faith. It encourages believers to treat one another with respect and love, regardless of their background or circumstances. A believer in Christ is a person who has faith in Jesus Christ as their savior and follows his teachings. To be a believer in Christ, a person must repent of their sins and make a commitment to follow Jesus as their Lord and Savior. This involves turning away from a life of sin and seeking to live according to Jesus' teachings as recorded in the Bible.

Those who support transgenderism and cross-dressing would also argue that it is also important to remember that the overall message of the New Testament is one of love and acceptance of all people, regardless of their gender identity or expression. They would then twist the text Matthew 22:39, Jesus teaches that the second greatest commandment is to "love your neighbor as yourself." This message of love and compassion should be at the heart of how we approach the issue of transgenderism and other matters related to identity and diversity. The phrase "love your neighbor as yourself" is a summary of Jesus' teachings about how believers in him should treat others. It means that we should show the same love, care, and concern for others that we have for ourselves. This includes showing compassion, kindness, and respect to those around us and seeking to do good to others as we would want them to do good to us. The commandment to love our neighbor as ourselves is a call to love and serve others selflessly without seeking anything in return. It is an expression of the love and compassion that God has for his people and that he desires us to have for one another. This phrase "love your neighbor as yourself" does not refer to our accepting a person transitioning from one gender to another or cross-dressing.

You see, you have to anticipate these replies and then have a ready response.

The Bible presents gender as a binary (two genders), with people being referred to as either male or female. The rarity of intersex individuals does not undermine the Bible's creation design of man and woman. Rather, it gives another example of creation "groaning" because of all that has resulted from human imperfection.

Romans 8:20-22 Updated American Standard Version (UASV)

20 For the creation was subjected to futility, not willingly, but because of him who subjected it, in hope 21 that the creation itself also will be set free from its slavery to corruption into the freedom of the glory of the children of God. 22 For we know that the whole creation has been groaning together in the pains of childbirth until now.

God did not create those whose sex is ambiguous at birth. This is simply another example of the result of sin and missing the mark of human imperfection.

Those who truly wish to follow Christ means that they are to die to themselves (Matt. 16:24), they are to be transformed by the renewal of their mind, that by testing you may discern what the will of God is, what is good and acceptable and perfect (Rom. 12:2), and no longer walking as they once did (Eph. 4:17-18). The modern concept of being "true to ourselves" will always end in failure. Genesis 6:5 and 8:21 says that fallen man is mentally bent toward evil. Jeremiah 17:9 tells us that imperfect humans have an unknowable heart that is treacherous.

If the binary of male and female is God's creation, which is how he designed humans, and we are expected to accept it, then our biological distortions of his creation by our redefining terms to fit our preferences would be in opposition to God, displeasing to him. The Bible is quite clear that men should not act sexually as women (Lev. 18:22; Rom. 1:18-32; 1 Cor. 6:9-10), that men should not dress like women (Deut. 22:5), and that when men and women embrace, obviously other-gendered expressions of identity it is a disgrace (1 Cor. 11:14-15). We do not have an inalienable right to do whatever we want with our physical selves. We belong to God and should glorify him with our bodies (1 Cor. 6:19-20).

1 Corinthians 6:19-20 Updated American Standard Version (UASV)

[19] Or do you not know that your body is a temple of the Holy Spirit within you, whom you have from God, and you are not your own? [20] For you were bought at a price; therefore, glorify God with your body.

In this passage, the apostle Paul is writing to the Christian community in Corinth and reminding them that their bodies are not their own. They have been purchased by God through the death and resurrection of Jesus Christ, and therefore they belong to God. Paul is urging them to honor God by treating their bodies with respect and using them in ways that honor God. This includes taking care of their physical health and abstaining from behaviors that would harm their bodies, such as sexual immorality or substance abuse. It also includes using their bodies to serve others and to further God's kingdom.

Edward D. Andrews

CHALLENGED SOULS 7 GENDER IDENTITY: Alternative Lifestyles—Does God Approve?

Gender Identity. The concept of identity popularized by Erikson (1959) is a description of eight stages of the life cycle during which we experience and express different styles of being a person. Identity combines the senses of who I am, what I do, and how I do it. The sense of identity may be inchoate, affective, and inarticulate in the young child, while the introspective adult may articulate precise descriptions of his or her identity. Gender identity is only a part of the whole sense of identity, yet at the same time it is a core component around which nongender aspects of identity are crystallized. Failure to achieve precise gender identity may impair the development of mature, complex adult identity, whereas the mature normal adult accepts gender identity as a given quality and elaborates other identity attributes.

Experience and Identity. Several aspects of personal experience must be identified and separated: the "me" experience, the "I" experience, and the "self" experience. Each is a part of the sense of identity but not necessarily gender-linked. The "me" experience refers to the sense of being alive, of possessing what happens to myself. Such experience is present probably in early infancy, later cognated upon, and then verbalized as the sense of me. The experience of me precedes and is distinct from the acquisition of sense of gender. The experience of "I" is the conscious appreciation of ego operations such as cognition, affect, and perception. That is, one experiences the sense of I am thinking, seeing, doing, feeling, deciding, acting. Again, the sense of I precedes and is distinct from the acquisition of sense of gender.

The term *ego* shall be construed operationally to describe mental operations—that is, cognition, perception, affect systems. Ego operations are experienced and directed. But ego operations are impersonal. We acquire different styles of ego operation that may become part of our identity formation, for example, "I am a fuzzy-thinking person" versus "I am a clear-thinking person." Ego styles are gender-linked. In a given culture males and females are differentially socialized in different styles of ego operations. We may say, for example, "You think like a woman" and thereby make an accurate observation of cultural influence on gender-linked ego style (Spence & Helmreich, 1978).

Self is the image of Who am I? It is a complex mental construction, including my ideal self or what I ought to be (the combined psychoanalytic ego ideal and superego), my desired self (a consciously constructed self-model), and my actual self (the observation of my person in action). Self-identity is neither innate nor epigenetic, as is true of me and I experiences. Rather, self-identity is learned, constructed, formulated, modified, and elaborated on throughout life (Gergen, 1971). Gender plays a major role in the development of self-identity. One can experience me, I, and ego operations apart from a sense of gender, but one does not experience self apart from a sense of gender.

It is obvious that sexual impulse, desire, and behavior are entwined with gender identity. Sigmund Freud interpreted sexuality as a basic determinant of identity. However, a century of research has demonstrated that sexuality is a reflection of gender identity rather than a determinant. That is, sexuality is acted out in terms of impulse, arousal, desire, and action on the basis of one's gender-identity formation (Stoller, 1968).

Anatomy and Destiny. A major question is raised by the obvious differences between male and female appearance, behavior, and role functions. Is this biological determinism or cultural artifact? It is appealing to assume that innate biological instincts account for male-female differences. In animal species we observe highly complex social behavior that is gender-linked. However, the biologic determinants of behavior shift with animal complexity; basic instincts are the same in human, monkey, pigeon, or worm. These generate drives, which become less directive as we ascend the phylogenic ladder, so that when we reach the level of humans, instinctual drive stimuli no longer determine specific behavioral complexes.

An example of this is the sexual instinct. The amoeba reproduces asexually at a predictable rate of fission. The earthworm has both male and female sex organs and copulates with another earthworm by matching male and female genitalia in random fashion. Frogs and birds mate only during a mating season, with gender-linked stereotyped courtship behavior and with a partner for the season. Higher mammals, such as the gorilla, form generational families, choose specific mates, mate during estrous seasons, and care for the young within the family structure. Young monkeys who are reared apart from the mother do not successfully copulate or care for their own young. In the human sexuality may never be expressed, in that celibate persons may live a normal and psychologically healthy life without significant sexual experience. Or persons may use sexual behavior to quell loneliness, anxiety, or conflict without experiencing any sexual pleasure. At the same time human sexual behavior is not necessarily linked to reproductive mating.

To conclude, in terms of biologic principles we cannot appeal to differences in male and female instincts to account for male-female variations in behavior per se.

The influence of genetic variation and hormonal influences on behavior must be considered. Persons with abnormal gender chromosomal patterns may exhibit genetic defects of deformations of skeleton or muscle formation. But their behavior may not differ from that of persons with normal gender chromosomes. If we administer sex hormones to a person, what will happen? In the average person, nothing. However, in some experiments, if one administers hormones to homosexual persons, they increase their homosexual activity level. That is, sex hormones increase the drive stimuli but do not change the sexual orientation of the person. Clearly then, gender behavior, including sexual behavior, cannot be accounted for primarily on biological grounds (Money & Musaph, 1977).

Facets of Gender Identity. The development of identity is biopsychosocial. We can truly speak of psychosexual identity, but more accurately we should speak of psychogender identity, since sexuality is an expression of gender sense. Eight variables contribute to psychogender identity (Money & Ehrhardt, 1972).

Variable 1: Chromosomal Gender. In the normal pattern the female has an XX sex chromosome pattern, the male an XY. In genetic abnormalities there may be five to six sex chromosome gene patterns, each giving rise to different clinical syndromes and involving different hormonal, musculoskeletal, and genital patterns and different levels of sexual potency. Yet a person with a female chromosome pattern may be born with male-appearing genitalia, be reared as male, and behave as male, and vice versa. The sex chromosome pattern obviously does not determine gender behavior.

Variable 2: Gonadal Gender. This refers to the presence of either testes or ovaries. In the embryo the human is bisexual, and under hormonal influence one set withers and the other grows. Yet in some cases of aberrant chromosomal and/or hormonal influence, the external genitalia may develop of one gender while the gonads are of opposite gender. Thus an infant may be born with female-looking genitals along with well-developed undescended testicles, or vice versa. Again, the primary gonads do not determine gender orientation or behavior.

Variable 3: Hormonal Gender. Males and females do have distinctive hormonal systems, produced by both the gonads and other body organs. Malfunction or disequilibrium in the hormonal systems may influence the male-female balance of hormones. In turn this may result in masculinization or feminization of body traits, such as voice, hair pattern, breast development, fat deposition, skeletal growth, and development of external genitalia in embryo. In children this may result in a chromosomal and gonadal male with a female hormone balance that causes feminization of body structure, or vice versa. Nonetheless, the person will act male or female in accord with that person's rearing, regardless of the hormonal balance or body habitus.

Variable 4: Internal Genitalia. This refers to the vagina and uterus in the female and prostate in the male. These internal organs develop in accord with embryonic hormonal patterns.

Variable 5: External Genitalia. These organs are the most visible evidence upon which we first assign gender. Yet they may be misleading. As noted, variations in chromosomal, gonadal, and hormonal variables may produce external genitalia that appear of one gender yet are opposite to all other previous gender variables. A male may not develop closure of the bilateral pubic genital tissues and appear to have a vulva. A female may have overdevelopment of the clitoris that looks like a penis. But the external genitalia do not determine gender identity.

In the case of transsexualism the person has the identity of one gender (I experience my identity as female) while having all the normal body attributes of the other gender (I live in a male body). In this instance the distinction between gender body attributes (biological) and gender identity (psychological) is clearly seen.

Variable 6: Gender of Assignment and Rearing. This refers to the label the parent gives the child as either male or female. Boys and girls are handled differently as infants by their parents. They are treated differently long before they can talk or cognate on their own gender identity. The child is socialized into a basic gender identity long before language acquisition. Such gender acquisition precedes language. The threshold for fixation of gender identity is about 18 months, while the point of no return for change in gender reassignment is about 30 months. After 4 years of age it is almost impossible to change gender assignment without severe psychological conflict in the child.

Variable 7: Core Gender Identity. This is the first basic sense of identity that is crystallized via cognition as part of self-identity. The child cognitively is able to state, I am a boy or girl. This appears to be organized as a cognitive construct between ages three or four. In contrast, the gender assignment has already been well established. It appears that when parents assign the child one gender (male) and treat the child as the other gender (female), the psychological conditions for transsexualism are created (I have been labeled a male but am treated as and expected to be a female). In psychotic regressive states we can observe similar confusion about core gender identity in patients who demonstrate no gender confusion in normal states. Persons with primitive character disorders similarly demonstrate gender identity confusion.

Variable 8: Gender Role Identity. This refers to the social patterns of appearance, behavior, and role performance associated with the sociocultural definitions of masculinity or femininity. There is probably some degree of psychological linkage between the sense of maleness or femaleness and behavior in masculine or feminine roles as defined by the culture. For example, in cultures with weak male roles the males demonstrate a higher incidence of identification with women, as in couvade (male pregnancy fantasies). One can experience a strong sense of maleness or femaleness, however, and not behave in traditional or expected gender-linked roles. For example, a feminine woman can be a police officer; a masculine man can knit doilies (Munroe & Munroe, 1977).

In the area of social gender roles there has been much confusion about the difference between gender identity and gender roles. The concept of androgyny has been promoted to do away with gender distinctions. This misses the point that gender identity is ineluctably a part of personal identity but that many social roles and behaviors need not be gender-linked (Sargent, 1977). The mature person with a secure gender identity is free to elaborate a wide variety of social role behaviors that become part of personal identity apart from gender.

Gender and Self-Identity. Although self-identity need not be tied to gender in many aspects, in another sense self-identity is always linked to gender. There are eight stages of psychological development of identity, according to Bemporad (1980). Each stage is not left behind but is incorporated into the next developmental level. Thus in the mature adult we continue to see reflections of each stage of identity.

Stage 1. In what is called an oral incorporative mode the newborn engulfs everything encountered. This style of relating to the world is to take it in and make it part of himself. The young infant does not differentiate between self and other. The lack of body boundaries, the timeless sense of fusion with the other, the experience of engulfing and being engulfed is reexperienced in adult life in sexual orgasm. The theme of incorporative identity is reflected in love play with nibbling or biting and in courtship with the primordial declaration: "I love you so much I could eat you up!"

Stage 2. Between 15 and 36 months the young child identifies the body as part of self, and body image becomes a major nidus of self-identity. Possession of body is possession of identity. The same motif is seen in adults who experience a sense of loss of identity when accident, surgery, or illness results in loss or immobilization of body parts. Where body is still a major source of self-identity and sexualized, the loss of genitalia (gonads, breasts) or sexual function may be experienced as a major loss of identity. The statement "I don't feel like a man or a woman anymore" reflects a sexualized fixation on body as a source of identity and of gender identity.

A bit later the child extends the body boundaries to objects, clothes, or playthings as body extensions. My things are my body, are part of me. Again, in adults we see identity rooted in possessions as a source of identity or gender identity reinforced through possessions: "I have a gun, ergo I am a male!" or "I have a house, ergo I am a woman!"

Stage 3. Between 3 and 5 the child differentiates self from other objects. There is generic identification with children of the same gender. Boys and girls reinforce gender identity by modeling and emulating behavior and social roles of the same-gender parent. Play helps the child to learn how to be an adult person. Identity is related to how one looks, acts, behaves. Playing house is modeling behavior that reinforces gender identity. Identity is developed in terms of social custom that differentiates men and women. Little girls cook, bake, and sew. Little boys pound nails and mow grass. This need not and should not be preparatory role behavior for adulthood, but some gender-linked role modeling is necessary to reinforce the sense of "I am becoming a man or a woman." This is identity through same-gender comparison.

Stage 4. Ages 5 to 7 is the oedipal period, in which identity development occurs through opposite-gender comparison. The child elaborates gender identity by modeling behavior of the same-gender parent with the opposite. The boy tries to behave with mother like father does. The girl treats father like mother does. Children will naturally emulate erotic and seductive behavior of the parent. Children act this way not because of infantile sexual strivings, as Freud suggested, but rather because they are modeling the sexy behavior of their parents. At this stage children need affirmation from both parents that these early strivings toward adult behavior are not bad and that in adulthood they will find mates to replicate the behavior of mother and father. Disapproval of either parent, fear of either parent, or failure to successfully identify with the parent of the same gender all lead to failure at this stage of identity development. In the view of some theorists, parents have, therefore, the potential to contribute to the development of a homosexual orientation. In such a view, homosexuality is not a problem of sexuality but a failure in maturation of identity development at the oedipal stage (Stoller, 1968).

Stage 5. In Latency, 7 to 12 years, the child elaborates personal identity via doing things. Skill acquisition enables the child to define personal abilities and ego coping style unique to him or her. Again, skill acquisition is in part linked to gender: learning male skills and female skills. But at this stage it is possible to also offer children androgynous skill acquisition not linked to gender but instead adding to development of unique individual skills and identity.

Stage 6. In adolescence the sense of self is heightened. Sexual drive stimuli are increased, and attraction to the opposite gender occurs. But what is the nature of the attraction? It is an exchange of mutual ideal images. The teenager falls in love with a projected image of an ideal, which is reciprocated. When the ideal image is tarnished by harsh reality, the puppy love dissolves. The attraction is reciprocated appreciation of an ideal self. When this is then eroticized, one feels a sexual attraction. Sexual interaction becomes a vehicle for reinforcement of self-identity.

Stage 7. In young adulthood a major transmutation of identity must occur from "what I do gives me identity" to "who I am gives meaning to what I do." That is, external attributes have given value to self-identity. Now the young adult must invest in internal attributes, an internal constructed sense of self, and identity apart from external exigencies. Failure to accomplish this task results in persons who seek others, sexually or not, to reinforce their own identity, self-esteem, value, and self-worth. So-called identity crises may occur in adults who lean on external definitions of identity and therefore lose their sense of self when those externalities diminish or disappear.

Stage 8. Mature adulthood involves the capacity to share one's identity with another. Mature love involves the capacity to retain one's own autonomy and identity but also acquire a shared identity with a partner. Marriage and sexuality can occur without sharing the intimacy of identity. Mature love involves "growing together" (Curtin, 1973). Here gender identity merges into a joint male-female identity of a marital pair.

The biblical observations that "male and female created he them" and "the two shall become one" represent the journey of psychogender development. The child begins with genderless fusion, acquires a gender identity, and moves on to an autonomous unique personal identity. But the mature adult shares gender identity with a mate of the opposite-gender identity in a new fusion that is a gender and sexual union, two unique self-identities, and a conjoint mutual marital identity. Thus there is the sense of paradox, in that identity is on the one hand profoundly rooted in a distinct sexual gender and on the other hand unites and transcends gender.

CHALLENGED SOULS 8
Finding Peace Amidst Chaos: A Guide for Today's Youth

Navigate the chaos of the modern world with our Christian guide for today's youth, exploring ways to find divine peace. Discover how a deep relationship with God, engaging in God's Word, active fellowship, and service can bring lasting tranquility in your life.

In today's world, where chaos and uncertainty seem to be the new normal, finding peace can often feel like a daunting task. The daily bombardment of disturbing news, the peer pressures of modern society, and the unique challenges that come with transitioning from childhood to adulthood can stir a whirlwind of emotions, confusion, and anxiety. However, as young Christians, we are not left without a guiding light and an anchor in these tumultuous times. Our faith in God and the timeless wisdom of His Word offers us the pathway to true peace amidst the chaos.

The Bible assures us in Philippians 4:7 that "the peace of God, which surpasses all understanding, will guard your hearts and your minds in Christ Jesus." This peace is not contingent on external circumstances but is anchored in the unwavering nature of God and His promises. So, how can you, as a young Christian, access and sustain this divine peace in a chaotic world?

Understanding God's Peace

To find God's peace, it's crucial to understand what it is and what it is not. God's peace does not necessarily mean the absence of problems or discomfort. Rather, it's an inner sense of calm, assurance, and trust in God, even amidst difficulties and chaos. It's the tranquility that stems from knowing God is in control and that He is working all things together for our good (Romans 8:28).

Cultivate a Deep Relationship with God

Building a deep, personal relationship with God is the cornerstone of finding His peace. This relationship begins with accepting Jesus Christ as your personal Lord and Savior, acknowledging your need for His grace, and deciding to follow His ways.

Prayer is a vital tool in building and sustaining this relationship. Philippians 4:6 urges us, "do not be anxious about anything, but in everything by prayer and supplication with thanksgiving let your requests be made known to God." Through consistent prayer, you cultivate open communication with God, share your worries, and receive His peace.

Immerse Yourself in God's Word

Reading and meditating on God's Word is an essential practice in finding peace. The Bible is a reservoir of God's promises, wisdom, and guidance. By studying it, you align your mind with God's thoughts, which results in peace. Verses such as John 16:33, where Jesus assures us that He has overcome the world, provide hope and peace during challenging times.

Foster Christian Fellowship

Surrounding yourself with other believers can help you maintain peace. Fellow Christians can offer support, encouragement, and spiritual insights that can fortify your peace. Participate actively in your local church, join Bible study groups, or engage in Christian youth organizations where you can grow together in faith.

Serve Others

Serving others in love is a powerful antidote to the chaos and self-centeredness of the world. Acts of service take our focus off our problems and allow us to experience the joy and peace of fulfilling God's commandment to love our neighbors (Mark 12:31).

Embrace God's Sovereignty

Realizing that God is in control, even when things seem chaotic, brings peace. Acknowledge His sovereignty in all situations and trust that He is capable of turning any situation around for your good.

Maintain a Lifestyle of Praise and Thanksgiving

Praise and thanksgiving keep our minds on God's goodness, thus fostering peace. Regularly express your gratitude for what God has done and continues to do in your life. Cultivate a heart of worship, praising God in songs and hymns.

Finding peace amidst chaos is a journey, not a one-time event. It requires an ongoing commitment to grow in your relationship with God, trust Him, and remain grounded in His Word. Remember, you're not walking this path alone; God has promised never to leave nor forsake you (Hebrews 13:5). Cling to Him, rely on His promises, and let His peace rule in your heart, regardless of the chaos around you.

Bibliography

Andrews, E. D. (2016). *HOMOSEXUALITY - THE BIBLE AND THE CHRISTIAN: Basic Bible Doctrines of the Christian Faith.* Cambridge, OH: Christian Publishing House.

Andrews, E. D. (2017). *THE OUTSIDER: Coming-of-Age In This Moment.* Cambridge, OH: Christian Publishing House.

Andrews, E. D. (2017). *TURN OLD HABITS INTO NEW HABITS: Why and How the Bible Makes a Difference.* Cambridge, OH: Christian Publishing House.

Andrews, E. D. (2017). *YOU CAN MAKE A DIFFERENCE: Why and How Your Christian Life Makes a Difference.* Cambridge, OH: Christian Publishing House.

Andrews, E. D. (2018). *40 DAYS DEVOTIONAL FOR YOUTHS: Coming-of-Age In Christ.* Cambridge, OH: Christian Publishing House.

Andrews, E. D. (2018). *LET GOD USE YOU TO SOLVE YOUR PROBLEMS: GOD Will Instruct You and Teach You In the Way You Should Go.* Cambridge, OH: Christian Publishing House.

Andrews, E. D. (2018). *THE POWER OF GOD: The Word That Will Change Your Life Today.* Cambridge, OH: Christian Publishing House.

Andrews, E. D. (2018). *WHY ME?: When Bad Things Happen to Good People.* Cambridge, OH: Christian Publishing House.

Andrews, E. D. (2023). *FAITHFUL MINDS: A Biblical and Cognitive Behavioral Therapy Approach to Mental Health and Wellness.* Cambridge, OH: Christian Publishing House.

Andrews, E. D. (2023). *LIFE DOES HAVE A PURPOSE: Discovering and Living Your Ultimate Purpose.* Cambridge, OH: Christian Publishing House.

Andrews, E. D. (2023). *MERE CHRISTIANITY REIMAGINED: Rediscovering the Faith for the 21st Century.* Cambridge, OH: Christian Publishing House.

Andrews, E. D. (2023). *UNSHAKABLE BELIEFS: Strategies for Strengthening and Defending Your Faith.* Cambridge, OH: Christian Publishing House.

Andrews, E. D. (2023). *WOKEISM: The Predatory Grooming of Your Children.* Cambridge, OH: Christian Publishing House.

Andrews, E. D., & Torrey, R. A. (2016). *Christian Living: How to Succeed in the Christian Life.* Cambridge, OH: Christian Publishing House.

D., A. E. (2017). *IS THERE A REBEL IN THE HOUSE?: Youth Overcoming a Rebellious Heart.* Cambridge, OH: Christian Publishing House.

Freeman, H. (2017). *WAGING WAR: A Christian's Cognitive Behavioral Therapy Workbook.* Cambridge, OH: Christian Publishing House.

Overton, T. (2018). *DEVOTIONAL FOR YOUTHS: Growing Up In Christ.* Cambridge, OH: Christian Publishing House.

Stalnaker, C. W. (2022). *FAITH ADRIFT CHRISTIANITY: How Can We Avoid Drifting Away from God?* Cambridge, OH: Christian Publishing House.

Williams, D. T. (2019). *THE YOUNG CHRISTIAN'S SURVIVAL GUIDE: Common Questions Young Christians Are Asked about God, the Bible, and the Christian Faith Answered.* Cambridge, OH: Christian Publishing House.

www.ingramcontent.com/pod-product-compliance
Lightning Source LLC
Chambersburg PA
CBHW022106040426
42451CB00007B/150